Across Continents

Across Continents

Mr. Govind Bhadresa

To order additional copies of this book, contact:
Xlibris Corporation
1-888-795-4274
www.Xlibris.com
Orders@Xlibris.com
68172

PREFACE

❮ ✤o✤ ❯

The discovery of new lands in the world began many centuries ago and increased in its tempo in the recent centuries. It began as early as the fourteenth century, and accelerated apace in the last couple of centuries. The pace accelerated even more in the last few decades. People of western nations like Spain, Portugal, France, Italy, Germany, Britain and others were venturing into different areas of the world, occupying and slicing up large areas of the land and claiming the booty in the name of the rulers of their own countries. Their pioneering and adventurous sprit led them eventually to every corner of the globe. Mass cruelties and even genocide was not out of the question if there was any dissension from the natives.

Despite the fact that there were many drawbacks for the explorers and they themselves had to face starvation, disease, animal and human enemies and many other discomforts, there were also many indisputable achievements that benefited the inhabitants and the land enormously.

The new of the newly acquired lands needed skilled and semiskilled workers. India, along with many countries from the east supplied the needed migrants to till the soil and perform other manual labor that would help to open out the new lands and of course the plunder of the land and the people. Many of the indentured laborers lost their lives in doing their duty.

East Africa was one of these lands. It included Kenya, Uganda, Tanganyika, Rhodesia, Abyssinia, and Zambia and many others. The land was divided by the victors, thus Kenya became a British Colony, Uganda a British Protectorate, while Tanganyika came under the tyranny of Germany.

The poor migrants who were fleeing the poverty and strife of India and other lands made a backbone on the backs of which rode the landlords, the white masters. They faced hostilities from man and beast, pestilence as well disease of an unbelievable variety. Some faced and went through a mass exodus as was ordered by Idi Amin in Uganda. It was a cruel imposed exile which in a long run produced a surprising and a good result for their progeny. Nevertheless, their industriousness and hard work produced an unprecedented success for themselves, their families, and even their newly adopted motherlands in Uganda and elsewhere.

Not unlike a spark that can start a disproportionate and enormously powerful fire, so also the spark from some of these families ignited the fire of development. Stories of the adventure that these men and women went through are legion and have been described by many a writer. The story of one of these families is described here. Like the spokes of a wheel that gives strength to the wheel, so also was each member of the family instrumental in the success of the particular family.

G.N.Bhadresa

KENYA

CHAPTER 1

≺ ৩০৬ ≻

KENYA

Rainforests of Kenya

Aberdare National Park was created in 1950. It is a part of the Aberdare Range of Mountains in Kenya being about 160 kilometers long, running in a north to south direction, forming the eastern boundary of the Great Rift Valley. It runs from the Kinangop Plateau to Laikipia Escarpment. It is often called the 'Nyandaruas', or the Sattima Range—Oldoinyo la Satima (mountain of the young bull) by the Kikuyu tribe that inhabit the area. One of the points of entry to the park is from the Central Province at Wandare gate. Central Province is a vital area for Kenya's economy. It is also of significance because of its location, politics, agriculture, tourism etc, and of course, its people.

It is a mountainous rainforest, where the rain falls as a downpour, continuously and incessantly with minimal letup. The sun shines in the daytime, every day and throughout the year. That makes it for a very hot and humid day, every day! It also encourages the growth of all varieties of flora and fauna. On a clear day the view of the mountains and valleys is spectacular but often the mist and rain blur it and make it surreal, giving it the appearance of an under water world. It is more than three thousand meters above sea level, making it rather cool in the mornings, quite warm in the day and bitterly cold at night. It is hot in the late afternoons as it lies on the Equator. The seasons are basically 'rainy' and at other times 'not so rainy'. It has many lakes. The greenery takes all forms, with huge and tall trees forming a formidable canopy above, overshadowing the wide variety of plant life that grows underneath on the ground. The greenery on the ground forms a thick green luxuriant carpet on the very uneven ground below. Marshland, with tussock grass growing in clumps every where, heather and bushes abound in the area. Not to be outdone by the abundant flora, the fauna consists of many kinds of animals, so much so that there is nowhere else in the world where the magnificent spectacle that nature reveals has its rival. The coolness and the darkness before the morning breaks has an eerie and somewhat scary feeling as all life is in slumber, but about to wake and start the day's activities. The sun begins to shine its warm and life-giving rays very early in the morning, and as they peep through the tall trees, they act as a signal for many creatures to open their eyes and start their activities of foraging, greeting others or start hunting. Satisfying hunger and procreation is paramount in their instincts. The rays become fiercer as the day progresses. By evening, sounds like the roars of lions, low growls of leopards, elephants, cheetahs, rhinos, wild buffaloes, as well as the screeching of birds become a cacophony that is an onslaught to the ear. The wild buffaloes are interesting in that while wallowing in all that mud, they urinate copiously and continuously all through the night! The sounds reach a peak by nightfall as the predators let their presence be known, while the hunted run to find refuge in a panic. The creatures in abundance in this region are elephants, rhinos, buffaloes, warthogs, a variety of deer like impalas, gazelles and dickdicks, cheetahs, leopards, servat cats, monkeys of all kinds, including the vicious baboons, vervet monkeys, colobus, macaque, cercopithicus etc., as well as over two hundred species of birds!

All of it make for a truly amazing and an unforgettable experience. For the tourist it is well worth a visit, even though it may be a long way around the world for some of them to travel to get to the area.

The Kikuyu believe that the Sun is taken down to the river in the evening, and is given a thorough wash making it presentable the next morning! It glows in all its glory between the mountains in the morning. Nature presents it with breathtaking colors as it surrounds the sun in all its glory at sunrise. Sunsets are also just as spectacular.

CHAPTER 2

❰ ❧0❧ ❱

Turbulent times in Kenya

In the late 1930s, times were becoming ominous for the whole world with a forebodings of a looming disaster. In Europe sabers were being rattled because of perceived threat by various countries such as Great Britain, France, Germany, Poland, Italy, Russia and many others, against the ones they considered foe, and the ominous start of World War II did not appear to be too far in the horizon. The clouds in the skies were darkening with foreboding. The devastating war indeed started soon after in 1939, with its indescribable toll of misery, loss of an untold number of human lives, involving not only men, but also women and children of these and many other innocent nations. Some of the countries were totally devastated. The tranquil slumber that the people of Kenya were under was also disturbed. Kenya was a colony of Great Britain, and the British built large Prisoner of War camps in the country, and imprisoned many prisoners captured in the war in these camps. One of these camps was based at Kiganjo. Most of the prisoners were Italians. It was said at the time that the Italians went one step forward and two steps backwards! They were gentle souls, and many came back after the war, as they had fallen in love with the country and its beautiful women. Some even married and formed families with the lovely African women. They established many missions of charity and compassion, which are in existence even today. The British were good to them, and allowed them considerable latitude in their movements. They were also given five shillings a week for sustenance. Not only that but they were also allowed to supplement their incomes by using the considerable talents that they had. As an example, they walked all the way into town, about eight miles away, and offered to do all kinds of work that required some skill. They repaired old watches and clocks that appeared useless to their owners. They also made remarkable toys, one of which was in the shape of a boat. A container with a wick was made under the front end of the boat. It was removable, and after filling it with kerosene and after lighting it, it was reinserted in the housing. The boat was then made to float on the water. It made a noise like an engine, being pushed by a small exhaust that came from the exhaust pipe that was made under it and opening out at the back. It was fascinating to see it go in circles in a basin of water. The little watercrafts enthralled many a child in those years.

CHAPTER 3

Mount Kenya

Mount Kenya is a volcanic mountain with three peaks. The central one, which is higher than the other two peaks that are on either side of it, is called Batian. The other two are called Nelion and Lenana. Batian seems to touch the skies as its lofty peak is at 17,058 Feet above sea level. The Kikuyu call it 'Kiri Nyaga'. The main peak along with the other two look down in all their majesty at the land truly blessed by Ngai, or Mungu, the God of the tribe. Wild life abounds in the area. It is not uncommon to see mighty elephants, bad tempered rhinos and wild buffalo grazing amicably but keeping their distance, and sharing the land. Smaller wildlife such as deer, variety of birds is also to be seen in the area. The land has a very rich and fertile soil, encouraging all forms of growth. As a consequence, it is very profitable to farm in the region. Thus the indigenous but poor people, and the settlers from Britain, raise cattle, grow many crops both above and below ground such as coffee, tea, maize etc. These crops grow in abundance because of the rich fertility of the soil as mentioned above. (Before independence, only white man was allowed to grow coffee!). Over the years, many towns cropped up in the area. They were Nyeri, Nanyuki, Karatina, Embu, Keregoya, Rumruti, Nyahururu (earlier called 'Thomsen's Falls'), Mweiga, Oljorok etc. The main town is Nyeri, where our story makes its exciting debut. The town forms the centre of activity for civil servants and others who work under the government, business, farmer co-operatives etc.

CHAPTER 4

❧❀❧

Treetops Hotel

On an afternoon in the nineteen thirties, a speck becomes visible on the horizon in a clear sky over the rainforest. As it comes into view one can discern four passengers in the small Cessna. They are the famous Brock Brothers surveying the land. They are the multimillionaires that own a chain of hotels in Kenya. They envisioned this area as a land of opportunity, and made up their minds to invest money into the project that was already taking shape in their minds. An area by one of the larger lakes was to be cleared and a hotel built on the large fig trees that abound in the region! Add to this, two artificial moons were to be constructed and salt spread daily on the land in an effort to attract all kinds of animals. A road coming from Nyeri was to be built. Tourists were to be brought here after they spent a night at the Outspan Hotel in Nyeri. Needless to say the hotel also belonged to the same brothers. The project went ahead, and it was a success beyond their wildest dreams.

Even now, after an overnight stay at the beautiful Outspan Hotel in Nyeri, the tourists are driven to the area in sturdy, four wheel drive vehicles called Landrovers. A white, tall and muscular hunter escorts the group. His uniform is rather interesting, in that he is dressed in khaki *in toto*—stockings, shorts, shirt, and waistcoat without sleeves, and a strap of bullets angled across his chest coming down from the shoulder. On his other shoulder he has a massive shot gun, which can bring down even an elephant! The road is muddy and treacherous, and the vehicles can only go a certain distance, after which the group has to go by foot. The hunter leads the party. There are quite a few shelters built along the way, as there is always a possibility that some wild animal could see the tourists as a threat and attack them. On reaching the hotel, ladders are dropped from above, so that the visitors can climb up to go to the hotel. On reaching the top, instructions are given with regards to the overnight stay there, after which the party is escorted to their various rooms. They are strongly advised not to leave windows, doors etc open, as the baboons that are always present in the area love to snatch cameras, handbags and anything else they can lay their hands on! On the top level is a large deck with sidings all around it, and on which one can walk around, and get a view that is simply breathtaking. It is also possible to see in all directions. From here wildlife can be seen on the ground, as well as on the trees. The giant trees and the greenery are seen well into the distance, but at times it is blanketed out by the mist.

Lights in all the rooms are dimmed, and a system of gentle bells rings at night to wake the sleepy heads, in case there is some unique animal that has approached the hotel and the opportunity of seeing them is not to be missed.

Dinner is announced by the ringing of a gong. The party is ushered into the dining room, which has four long tables. Mouth watering gastronomic delights cooked by the excellent chefs in the kitchen is presented. The tables themselves are unique. A dolly is built on the table and goes from one end of the table to the other. These dollies are on wheels that travel on rails that are fixed on the table. All food is sent down along the table by means of a moving platform that is on the wheels. Strong Kenya Coffee is available throughout the night helps the residents stay awake. There is a thick glass partition that separates the land from the onlookers. It feels as though the animals are so close that it gives one the eerie feeling that one can reach out and touch them. The wild buffaloes and rhinos stay around all night, while many other animals just appear transiently. It is something to see nature in the raw and appreciate the truly amazing spectacle of nature. It is remarkable to see the untrusting nature of some of these animals. After an overnight stay and a good breakfast, the party is sad and reluctant to leave this paradise of nature, as yet unspoiled by man in his ever reaching prowess.

The original Treetops Hotel was burned down during the Mau Mau rebellion, and a larger hotel was built across the lake. (Not to be outdone, the competitors have built another hotel not far from there. It is in the shape of a boat, and they have aptly called it 'The Ark' in memory of Noah, one would think).

It was while staying overnight at The Treetops Hotel that a young Princess named Princess Elizabeth from Britain became Her Majesty Queen Elizabeth II of Great Britain, Northern Ireland, and all the colonies as well as head of the Commonwealth. It happened at the time when her father, King George VI died of lung cancer. The Princess was informed of her father's passing while she was actually staying over night in a hotel that is on top of the trees! H.R.H. the Duke of Edinburgh, Prince Consort, was with her at the time. Thus it was a Princess that went up to The Treetops Hotel to spend the night and came down a Queen the next day. How romantic!

One may add that she is a true queen in the hearts of all her people. It is also the prayer of the people of the commonwealth and others that her reign will go on for a very long time.

❰❧❍☙❱

CHAPTER 5

❧❀○❧❦

The Town of Nyeri

The town of Nyeri is about 100 miles north-northeast from the hustling, noisy, throbbing capital city of Nairobi. The land takes a climb upwards from Nairobi to the green and tranquil 'White Highlands', going up to and beyond nine thousand feet! The road to Nyeri passes the towns of Thika, Saba Saba, (in Swahili, Saba is seven), Fort Hall, Maragua and Karatina. Maragua is where there is a big train junction, and from there the train runs parallel to the main road. The train has to have another engine joined to it, as it just cannot climb and go further without the help of another engine! Even then, the town of Nyeri could not be reached as the climb is too high. It is diverted to a small hamlet about eight miles away called Nyeri Station, or Kiganjo. From Kiganjo the train goes to Nanyuki where it makes its final stop. Nanyuki is at the base of Mount Kenya. Further up by road, one can go to Meru, Isiolo and further travel leads to the border of Ethiopia. This region is very dry, arid and uninviting, an ideal place where the British harbored Kenyatta, the first President of Kenya, in a place called Lodwar.

The approach road into Nyeri is from the south side coming from the capital. Upon entry, the road leading to the town turns east. Along this road, on the south side is The Nyeri Indian Primary School (now called the Temple School). The Hindu temple is further down the road. On the north side is a large football field. On the Southside of the Hindu Temple, is the Gurudwara, a sikh temple. After about three hundred yards, one turns north again, into the Dedan Kimathi Road. Dedan Kimathi was a hero in the Mau Mau rebellion. Going north for about three-quarters of a mile, one reaches the tower. It was built by the British in memory of King George V. The Tower has a chiming clock and also provides fresh cool water for many a thirsty mouth. The road,n reaching the tower the road forks. The branch on the left leads to Outspan Hotel and further on the superb and beautiful Ring Road. It passes the beautiful golf course which is on the left hand side. Residences along ring road are for the rich. The fork on the right leads to the Police Station. The same road after making many sharp and downward turns crosses the Chania River, then climbs up, where it once again forks, the right one leading to the Nyeri Prison, Prince of Wales Boarding School for the Whites, The Nyeri Station, while the left one leads to Mathari or Consolata Mission, which is run by Italians. If one turns right instead of turning left on the Dedan Kimathi Road, one is led to a residential area, an abattoir, and further down to the Provincial General Hospital.

While it cannot be disputed that one of the claims to fame by Nyeri was that of a Princess that became a Queen while visiting it, making it like a fairy tale, there was another as momentous a reason. None other than Lord Baden Powel retired here, and in fact died in Nyeri. He was the founder of the Boy Scouts movement—a movement that is now recognized worldwide. There is nowhere in the world where the great movement is not known. It helps in the growth of youths into great and mature people. Parallel movements like girl guides, sparks etc have also started for the girls.

It is now one hundred years since the movement had started.

Lord Baden Powell of Gilwell (Robert Stephenson Smyth Baden-Powell, Ist Baron Baden Powell of Gilwell)—1857-1941—lived and retired in the Outspan Hotel He lived out his days here. All his memorabilia are in a hut called 'Paxtu', which is attached to the hotel. His funeral was massive, but in later years Britain rewarded her undisputed hero by moving his body to the cemetery which is next to Westminster Abbey in London.

Town of Nyeri

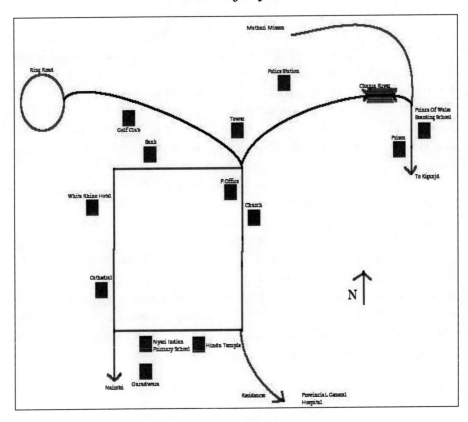

It should also be pointed out that two of the Presidents of Kenya came from Nyeri, They were both Kikuyu. The first one put up a glorious fight for freedom and won. The country was granted independence in 1953 by Britain when the shatters were truly broken. His name was Jomo Kenyatta. The last one—the one who is in power at the moment is called Mr. Mwai Kibaki. The face of this beautiful land is changing under the rule of the latter, wiping out all corruption as well as violence restoring the wealth and friendliness of this great land. The Italians run the missions, where they have hospitals, nursing homes, printing press, church etc. They are not short of money, as they own many square miles of this area that grows excellent coffee.

The history of coffee is rather interesting. The original coffee crop growing in Kenya was totally destroyed by a parasitic infection. The seeds were imported from South America. Hence in fact the coffee growing in Kenya now is Colombian Coffee!

As the northern part of Nyeri is approached, one sees an old church on the east side of the road. It has been there for many years. Many local people are ignorant and do not know what a church is, and the rumor was that a ghost of Jesus Christ lived there, and came out at night! It was considered to be rather scary by many.

There are many shops in Nyeri, a large number owned by Asians. A man called Nanji Meghji Bhadresa owns one of the shops. It is near the post office, and is at the top end and on the West Side of the street. It started as a women's tailoring store and was called 'Ladies Tailoring House'. In the earlier days, it was mainly a store that made made-to-measure clothes for ladies. These women were the immigrants that had a lot of money. They were often referred to as 'Europeans'. In the later years, it was a general store that had everything, and that means everything. Watches, clocks, bedding, material for purchase, televisions etc., and the repair of all these articles was also offered. If a thing was not available in this store, then it was more than likely not to be found in Nyeri. It happened quite often that while the other stores were not busy at all, this one was very busy. As a consequence, the wealth of the owners increased geometrically.

Mr. Nanji Meghji Bhadresa's story figures prominently. We will delve into the exciting story, which really is a family saga, a little later.

CHAPTER 6

Asian Immigration

The British had plans to build a railway line from the port city of Mombasa to the interior of Kenya and beyond into Uganda. They called it 'East African Railways and Harbors (EAR&H for short)'. Roger Whitaker has immortalized it by the lyrics of one or two of his songs. The famous singer was in fact born in Kenya. The railway was to run from Mombasa to Nairobi, where it would divide, one tract going north via Thika, Nyeri and on to Nanyuki. The other one would go from Nairobi, northwestwards, onto Naivasha, Gil Gil, Nakuru, Mbale, on into Kisumu and further on into Uganda, where it went to Jinja, Kampala and Entebbe. The last one was at the end of the line. The British had a large army base in Gil Gil. For the construction of the rail lines, indentured skilled and semiskilled workers were required. They advertised it in the newspapers in India, and as a consequence there was a flood of applications from people looking for a better life. Immigrants came from Punjab, Maharashtra, etc., but the largest number that emigrated was from Gujarat. India at that time was a land of poverty and misery and people were looking for opportunities elsewhere. Soon the word spread like wildfire that East Africa was a land of milk and honey and wave after wave of all forms of artisans, mostly from India followed.

The land that is East Africa is a fairly easy approach by sea from the West Coast of India. Apart from the short and direct access, the Trade Winds were also a great help in the travel between the two land masses. In fact many Indians sailed in unstable dhows, and if the winds changed its direction then even if they saw the land in the distance, but by sheer bad luck, if the winds changed, then they would not arrive at the same spots some weeks or months later!

Historically people throughout the world were obsessed with finding a route to India, discovering America and the Caribbean Islands only by chance; thus Christopher Columbus calling the people in the land that he came across as Red Indians, because he thought he was in India and called the people Indians! In 1497 Vasco da Gama found the sea route to India. In fact he only had to get to the coast of East Africa and the sailors that plowed the ocean in the area were happy to show him the way to India!

CHAPTER 7

Meghji Ghela Bhadresa

Aong with the hoard that came from India was a man called Megjibhai (Bhai-brother, often referred to as Meghjibapa, bapa-old dad). He had sharp, intense brown eyes, was short in stature, about five feet three inches, somewhat kyphotic, dressed in a typical Gujarati dress—a white turban that goes around in circles on top of the head, an almost totally bald head in his case. The turban is twisted on itself, and is about five yards long. It is worn horizontally. White long sleeved shirt with a waistcoat on top. White jodhpurs rather like what the British wore when they went riding on horses. He was rather finicky in his dress and appearances and the kids just loved him. All the clothing was white. He carried all kinds of small trinkets and foodstuffs like gram seeds in his pockets to win the heart of the little fellows that seemed to surround him constantly. At times he would go to the market and buy a whole sugar cane. He would bring it home, and skin it and cut into pieces, and then he gave out the pieces to all. Many mouths appreciated the sweet pieces. He had a sharp knife to do the job. In fact, he was also the proud collector of swords.

Unfortunately he had no business sense at all. He bought a watermill in Thika, and went bankrupt some months later! Later he started a bus service that ran from Thika to Nairobi and back. Even that was a loss, and eventually he went back to India, to appear once again in Kenya many years later.

CHAPTER 8

❖

Nanji Meghji Bhadresa

Mr. Meghji Ghela's son, Nanjbihai, immigrated to Kenya some years after Meghjibhai came to Kenya. He came from Ranavav, Gujarat State, in India. He was a very intense man, short, about 5 Foot 5 Inches in height. He reveled in his attire, which was a smart long sleeved shirt, khaki pants with a red leather belt around his waist, and a pocket watch of which he was rather proud. He would often take it out in company, and either check the time or wind the little beauty while the observers stared with envy. He was very upright, had a high standard of morals, and would not deviate from them. He would look down on anyone that would not agree with his views. Unfortunately, he developed a habit of talking out loud, and even shouted at times, so much so that quite often he could be heard from a distance. His grasp of English was rather poor as he addressed or talked about everyone in the female gender. To listen to him was hilarious at times, but nobody dared to point it out to him about the glaring and rather comic mistake. He referred to everyone as 'she' or 'her', male or female!

He started to work for an uncle in Nairobi. The hardships he, along with many other workers in the firm had to endure were unbelievable. He was a tailor and would have to start sewing army uniforms, which were made for the British soldiers, early in the morning. They would start at eight in the morning and work till ten at night! Cutting all the thick material with big scissors before starting to sew the pieces gave him large bunions on the base of his thumbs on the outer aspects. The food that was given to the workers was limited in amounts and was given only once a day. It was given in measured amounts consisting of three chapattis and a small container of dahl per day! Dahl is an Indian dish rather like soup.

Sometime later he quit this job and moved to the town of Thika where he started his own business. In Thika his wife gave birth to two sons. Later in Nyeri he had three boys. He thus fathered five boys.

Zaverben, his wife, was a child bride. The marriage took place when she was eleven years of age. He had a beautiful heavy necklace of gold made for her before he left the country. The necklace is a continuous source of hard feelings, as everyone who has it at the time seems to think that it belongs to that individual. He had left it with his step mother for safekeeping. She gave it to her favorite daughter, who now thinks it is hers, and now even denies it ever being in her possession. After marriage, according to Hindu custom, the young bride returns to her parent's household, and joins her husband's family later when she is thought to be mature. It was some years later that he had sent for her to come to Kenya and join him.

They settled in Thika where he had started his tailoring business. In Thika, the first two of the five children, as mentioned above, were born. It is said that lions roamed the railway station at the time. The eldest was called Jamnadas, and the second son was called Govind.

They were in Thika only some three or four years when another move was made. He had heard that another town called Nyeri, which further north and not too far—about sixty miles away, had even better pickings. He started his business venture once again in Nyeri. His other three children were born in this town. Their names were Tulsi (also called Jenti, or Tarachand), Maganlal, and Ramniklal.

In Nyeri, he proved to be an astute businessman, and the success that followed him was phenomenal. He started to invest his wealth in real estate, and eventually owned about ten buildings in Nyeri and one in Nairobi. He ventured into buying a piece of land that was in the 'White Highlands'. The area was reserved for 'Whites', and he had to go through unbelievable hassles before it could be approved for his purpose. He built a large two storey building there and called it 'Bhadresa Building'. He was hoping to move his business there, but at the last minute he realized that it was not an ideal site for carrying out business, and in fact never moved there. However, there were many nice apartments upstairs, while on the main floor there were many shops, one of them occupied by KANU, the first political party of Kenya, called the Kenya African National Union. It had to be rent-free for them, as they never offered rent! He always dressed smartly, and was often heard humming his favorite tunes from Indian movies. It was an era when motorized vehicles had started to appear on the scene. His first car was called an International. It was a wagon that was open at the back and sides. On both sides there were boxes for keeping tools etc. As the side was open, one could sit on the boxes, and hold onto the bodywork with dear life, and enjoy the fresh air that flew past. It was truly exhilarating. His love for Indian movies often led him to collect a group of people and drive down with them to Nairobi, which was a hundred miles away, just to see a movie! He came across Kagero, a man with treamendous driving abilities and mechanical prowess, and he hired him. Kagero's job was to keep all cars in good running order ensuring that all the mechanics were in good order. It included the car's suspension, engine, bodywork, brakes, lights, gear systems etc. He had to make the parts that were not available himself by using his ingenuity! His work became more extensive as the family was to acquire two more vehicles over time. He was also a chauffeur for the family.

One day when it was dull and stormy, Nanjibhai developed an urge to go and see an Indian movie in Nairobi. The city was one hundred miles away from the village of Nyeri. He collected his friend, a Mr. Narshi Pancha Shah, and his own son Govind for company. Kagero was to drive the group to Nairobi and back on the same day. The car was the famous International mentioned earlier. The group reached Thika, when the engine started to splutter. The skies turned dark and ominous. The town of Thika was just passed, and the evening was giving way to the night. Eventually the engine just stopped. Kagero went out, and removed the carburetor. He cleared all the holes and replaced it. Then, after attaching it, he bent over and blew on it with some force with his mouth. It did the trick, but after a couple of miles, the same happened. Out goes Kagero, and repeats the process. It went once again, and quit again after a couple of miles. After the third attempt, he just gave up, and the group had to spend the night in the car. Lions could not be seen, but their scary roars could be heard all night. In the movie was the famous actress called Lila Chitnis, and the famous song was 'tumine mujko prem sikhaya, soye huve hridayko jagaya'—meaning—'you taught me to love, and woke up this sleeping heart'. Lila Chitnis eventually emigrated and retired in California, and died at the ripe old age of 90!

CHAPTER 9

Bewitched in the village of Ranavav

Picture a small village in the state of Gujarat in India, called Ranavav. It probably means a small lake belonging to the local chieftain. It is a dry, dusty town, unhealthy, with open sewers. Emaciated dogs, cows and other domesticated animals, as well as monkeys, pigs, goats and other animals roam freely in the streets. In this town even toilets are a luxury because of their scarcity.

In this village, three little boys were playing in front of a house at one time. They were Jamnadas, Govind, and their uncle Keshavji. (brother of Nanjibhai). A woman who is well known in the village as a wicked witch was seen coming towards them. Her name was Kamar, who has cast evil spells on many a resident of the village, with disastrous consequences. Grandma sees her coming, and shouts at the kids ordering them to come into the house immediately. Govind and Keshavji, being obedient, listen to her and ran into the house. Jamnadas, being his stubborn self, and also acting out his usual defiant self, stood his ground and stayed put where he was. The witch did a spell on him, and he was never his own normal self again. His life was doomed after the curse. Soon after, he had diarrhea, vomiting, fevers etc. All forms of treatments were tried to no avail. One day a 'Fakir' (a sage) was passing through the village. He was told the story and asked if he would kindly see the afflicted boy. After seeing him, he came to the conclusion that the case affecting the boy was very serious, but reassured the family that he would undertake to treat him. He said he would bury seven seeds of 'mung' in the local cemetery, and on the next day, if these became six then there was hope for the boy. If they stayed at seven, then the boy was doomed and he would wash his hands off the case. As luck would have it, there were six the next day, and he agreed to treat the boy. He took the boy into the bathroom, and requested that boiled water be brought in. He bathed Jaman with it, and at the same time beat the boy with a 'dhoko', which is rather like a baseball bat. It is said that the screams emanating from the bathroom were that of Kamar, the witch, promising to get out of the boy's body. Afterwards, he made an amulet, and had the boy wear it around his neck. He was to wear it all his life. Even in the years to come, if he ever had to take off the amulet for some reason or other, e.g. for changing the decaying thread, etc., then his headaches, strange and odd behavior, etc would come back. Despite all this, he exhibited a personality disorder throughout his life. As an example one night he started to sing and dance on a bed with lantern in his hand. The lantern was lit. He did it with gusto. It was very dangerous and could easily have caused a fire!

He was to continue his strange behavior until his last days, which was many years later, when he collapsed and died, without anyone knowing as to what the cause of death was.

We will go into the story further at a later stage.

CHAPTER 10

⟨∞0∾⟩

Jamnadas

The children were growing up in this little town called Nyeri. Jamnadas was no exception, and being the eldest, he was presumed to be more responsible than any of the other children.

For education beyond Grade VI, he was sent to Nairobi as further education was not available in the little town. He obtained admission in the Government Indian High School in the city of Nairobi. For accommodation, he was to stay at his uncle's shop. After rising, doing his morning chores and eating breakfast, he would have to walk to school, which was located about a mile away from his residence. The school was located in an area called Ngara. The walk involved crossing a dirty and muddy stream that was about halfway to school. It carried the town's sewage also, and negotiating it involved walking carefully on the stones that were interspersed amongst the dirty water.

Soon after starting school in Nairobi, Jamnadas was not interested in any form of education, or even attending school. He collected like-minded individuals and started his and their nefarious activities. He collected friends and played cards with them all day by the river. Then he, along with his gang went to town to steal. They would approach parked cars, and if the owners were not about then out would come all the tools of the trade, and they would start to remove lights, mirrors, decals or anything else that was removable. The collection would then be offered for sale on the black market—an activity that turned out to be quite profitable. One day they were involved in this pursuit and did not notice that there was a large dog in the car. The dog started to bark ferociously, so much so that the gang took off in fright. From that day on he decided to discontinue the activity, and employed others who would go and do the job for him! At one time, he had sold a small motorcycle to one of his teachers and was bursting with pride about it as he narrated it to his brother! He also had a small handgun in his possession when he left school. Disposal of all his possessions was done in a cunning manner, in that all the stuff was buried in the ground in Nyeri, and after taking some friends with him for a walk, the treasure was discovered and

the surprise of the find by all was noted with satisfaction by him, as no one had
in fact noticed the trick.

He had to leave school before finishing it, as he was needed rather badly in
the shop. He joined the business and he in fact turned out to be quite an astute
salesman, and was quite a success in a short time. He was smartly dressed, with a
nice bright but conservative shirt, with armbands that would hold the shirtsleeves
up precisely, and pants matching exactly his shirt and shiny black shoes. He had
jet-black hair, somewhat raised, parted on the side, and made smooth and shiny
by large amounts of 'Brylcream'. He also sported a handsome moustache. He
was not very tall, about five feet five inches. The shop had to be expanded as the
business was growing. Later he was to add a printing press, a cinema, and one
of the major hotels in Nyeri (The White Rhino Hotel) to the business. He was
forever fidgety, and could not sit still for a minute. When there was no business
to be done, then he would go around the shop, both inside and outside, and clean
vigorously with a large duster, called a 'japatiyu'. Business is business, right?
There are no ethics in it as it would appear, but there is an unwritten law that there
is a fine line which is undefined. It should never be crossed, but it was crossed
as you will see as we follow the ins and outs of the following cases.

There were many customers that visited the shop but had no intention to
buy anything. They were just browsing and see some articles that looked rather
interesting. He would entice the customer to buy it, even if he did not have any
money—it did not matter. A bystander, who did not even know the customer,
would be asked to sign as a witness. It was often accomplished and the article
was sold. However, problems arose when the customer could not afford to make
the payments. The witness was sued to recover the money! The number of cases
built up that way was unbelievable. In fact there were two lawyers in town who
competed against each other to obtain his business. The authorities heard of it
and were obviously concerned. They felt that something more drastic ought to
be done as just warning him about it fell on deaf ears. One day a Jeep appeared
at the shop with four army officers in it. He was escorted to his house, and his
passport that he had in his home was taken from him. It was then torn up, and
after being allowed to change his clothes, he was escorted to Nairobi Airport
and from there deported to India. In fact there were a total of eight deportees in
that particular airplane; one of them even was a Medical Doctor!

While in India, the group even went to see Mrs. Gandhi, the Prime Minister
of India. She could offer nothing but sympathy. He phoned his younger brother
Govind who was studying Medicine in Liverpool, England at the time. He was
told that he should come to England where his business acumen could be very
useful. He managed his way to Liverpool and started business there. He bought

a typewriter on which he was busy typing every day till 3 or 4 in the morning! He had to share his room with Maganlal at that time, and his constant typing sure drove Maganlal crazy. Despite being told of his annoying habit, he never listened, so Maganlal threw him and his typewriter out of his room. The story went around in Kenya that Govind had thrown his older brother out of the house! At one time he looked very thoroughly into a taxi business in St. Helens, but he decided against buying the firm that was for sale. He eventually decided that Liverpool was too small for him, and said he would move to London very soon. Everyone breathed a sigh of relief.

He moved to London with a lot of money in his pockets—the money that he was able to import from Kenya, as the Government, though they deported him, let him collect his money from the old country for some years. He bought four laundromats in the East End of London. It was an all cash business, and he prospered once again. If anyone made a mistake and visited him, he would immediately take the visitor to the laundromats where he would request them to count the money along with him. Later he started to buy condemned properties and rent these out at outrageous prices. He also started a notebook in which he noted the names, addresses as well as other details of all the eligible girls and boys in the country. In this manner he had compiled a huge list. Because of it, he was instrumental in arranging many marriages in the community. It was a service that was truly appreciated by all concerned.

There was a time when he thought his younger brother Govind, who was a Medical student at the time, was too proud just because he possessed some certificates. An idea came to him and he started giving out certificates! He would charge 21 guineas per certificate for this service, but he would give out every fifth or sixth certificate free! Any person who wished to buy a certificate from him would inform him verbally as to who he was, and what he did, such as a garbage collector, a tailor, a shopkeeper etc. He would give a certificate to that person to that effect and confirm this fact. In fact his business was so popular that at times there were queues outside his house with people who wished to buy the certificates that would be issued by him! Some of his certificates are displayed in faraway lands, even as far away as some shops in India! The self inflated owners would have them nicely framed, prominently and somewhat proudly displayed on a prominent wall in their place of business, maybe along with a picture of God or Goddess, which is not uncommon in India. It is needless to mention that there was no examination of any kind involved.

He became an expert at producing excellent printing, and the results looked very authentic. Unfortunately he proceeded into other illegal activities, e.g. printing paper money and passing it on to the unsuspecting public. He was very successful at this venture. Later on he went into printing passports. He had friends in the Passport Dept. in the Government, and they would authenticate the passports printed by him by signing and stamping with a stamp of the appropriate authorities. He was caught, and had to spend six months in Brixton Prison. After his release, he was told that he would have to return to the prison if he continued his illegal activities. The notice was useless, as, on his release, he continued his illegal activities unabated.

Unfortunately, he collapsed one day at home. He was admitted in a Neurological Hospital, where he became unconscious, and unfortunately died there. Cause of death was not clear. It was said that he had septicemia. Some thought that he had died in mysterious circumstances.

It was interesting to see him during his time in London. He increased his weight and became a somewhat well built man. He started with some form of allergy in the nose, for which he took antihistamines without avail. He saw consultants in Rodney Street in Liverpool (Which is the equivalent of Harley Street in London), who were quite happy to empty his pockets. He had some ineffective surgeries carried out in the offices of these specialists. It made no difference to his suffering. On moving to London, he continued to see the specialists in Harley Street, who again carried out further surgeries. At one time one of the specialists had inserted a piece of plastic to cover a perforated nasal septum. The foreign substance did not stay in for long as it was blown out with some force when he had a sneeze at one time.

He led a very colorful life. He always dressed immaculately with a fresh flower in the lapel of his jacket. He was well groomed. He drove a Volkswagen Jetta, and on the center of the dashboard he had the picture of Jalaram, one of the saints of India. His driving was erratic, and he had no respect for traffic signs or signals. He was often seen going the wrong way on one-way streets! Had he lived, he would have the pleasure of seeing his children and grandchildren, all doing well.

While in London, it is said that he opened a 'numbered account' in Switzerland where he sent deposited all his money. Unfortunately he did not inform any member of his family the account number or any details, and to this day no member of his family has received any money from the account, being unable to access the account as they did not know the number.

He was a legend in many ways, and his passing left a void in many a heart. He could be sincere, hard working, very friendly and displayed Solomon's wisdom at times.

CHAPTER 11

Vidhata, the Goddess

One of the intriguing beliefs amongst Hindus is that Vidhata, the Goddess, appears at night on the sixth day of a child's birth. She writes a child's future on his forehead at birth. She is beautifully dressed and has delicate bells tied to her ankles. Her walk is very exciting, and the jingles from her anklets are heard with a faint 'chum, chum, chum', becoming louder as she approaches. The rhythmic and repetitive sound becomes quite loud when she is closer and can be quite frightening. She writes the whole destiny of the child on his forehead—as to how rich he will be, or how poor, how educated, and how much of a success in his life etc. It is said that once she has written all this, and whatever she has spelled out cannot be altered. Thus it is said that a personality is already formed at birth. It may lead one to conclude that a particular person's destiny is beyond his or her control.

CHAPTER 12

⊰ ✍⊙✍ ⊱

Govind's Destiny

Govind grew up in his paradise they call Nyeri, with not a care in the world. He had a large family with a doting father and mother. His father bought him a new bicycle every year, mostly because he would outgrow the older model.

He made satisfactory grades, but they were by no means fantastic. However, his bravado at times was excessive. For example, at one time he gathered about four boys, and made them sit on various parts of the bicycle, making them as comfortable as possible, with himself as the driver. The team then went hurtling down about fifteen steps that were in the front of the school on the bicycle. There was another time when some magicians had come to school, and as part of the show, ate some Gillette shaving blades. Not to be outdone, Govind collected some friends on the next day, and did precisely that—ate some shaving blades after cutting them into pieces! It was lucky that he and or the other accomplice who was his friend did not come to any major harm.

It is very easy to underestimate the great teachers that a student can come across. It is no less than like a shooting star that in passing leaves a bright unforgettable ray of a shining light in the mind of the child. Such a teacher was a Mr. Gandhi, who in fact taught by doing. One day he sent the students out to measure the school, the size of the compound, and the driveway etc. He had them draw it according to scale after obtaining all the measurements.

Govind was visiting him one evening. It was approaching sunset and the evening was getting gradually dark, but not in Mr. Gandhi's house. The only other house that had electricity at the time was that of a rich man called Mr. Osman Allu, who had a noisy large motor in his garage. It punctured the peace and tranquility of the night like a needle that makes a hole in a full-blown tube. However, it was even more disturbing the night it was not on! Mr. Gandhi had collected discarded metal boxes from the post office, and put in different solutions in them. By means of fine wires, different solutions in the boxes, and safety pins that acted as switches, he was able to produce electricity, and was able to light the house! Amazing! Another time he made a globe of the world from *papier maché* and glue, and making a form from cement. It was unfortunate that this gentleman had a better financial offer from Abyssinia, and although he left, he left an indelible mark in his student's minds.

The other teacher was called Mrs. Mahan. She was a great teacher, and expected all her students to do well. However, she had a habit of visiting various families in the afternoons and she loved to indulge in gossip. She would discuss many of the children that were in her class with their families, which sometimes made it a little embarrassing for the students. She was also the sister of the famous Mr. Kapila, who was instrumental in obtaining the release of Mr. Kenyatta. Jomo Kenyatta had the honor of becoming the first president of the republic of Kenya.

It was interesting in that in the 1950s and early 60s, Kenyatta was held prisoner in a place called Lodwar, a deserted region in northern Kenya. Sir Patrick Renison was the Governor at the time. In his speech he called Kenyatta the leader of darkness and death. The British, in a clever maneuver, changed the Governor soon afterwards, as Kenyatta was to be released in the ensuing days. As noted above, he became the first President of Kenya in 1963.

One of the lawyers involved in the case himself was charged for bribery and had to spend sometime in jail. Unfortunately, starting with the first president and the ones that followed could not stop the deluge of corruption, and they even partook in the disaster and evil human pursuit, with the result that the country is still in poverty even now. The largest slum in the world as a consequence is to be found in Kenya, specifically Nairobi.

CHAPTER 13

❮℘o℘❯

Govind's life in Kenya

One afternoon Govind had just finished school for the day and was sauntering off home, when he came across a column of ants on the ground. These were the so-called army ants. As a dare, and also because he was unable to resist a challenge, he put his bare foot on the column. Soon they were all over him, and their bites of formic acid are to be suffered once to know how painful they are. Panic-stricken, he ran straight home. He was screaming as he reached the courtyard where his mother was having a *tete-et-tete* with other ladies. She saw Govind, and immediately assessed his plight. She unclothed him completely, and dragged him to the water pump that was present in the yard. She opened out the faucet and made him stand under the cold water. She was so mad with him that as soon as the shower was done, she took him by the hand and flung him onto the concrete floor. As soon as Govind was up, she held him again and repeated the process. Govind was bleeding all over, but it did not arouse any pity in her or in any of the people that were watching. She eventually got tired, the night was approaching, and as she also had other chores to attend to, so she relented and returned to her them.

The years passed and when he was twelve a decision had to be made for his further education, as the education Grade VI—at Nyeri had come to an end. He was sent to Nairobi to follow in his elder brother's footsteps. His dad, Nanjibhai, drove him to Nairobi where he met his uncle, a Mr. Laxmidas Khimji Bhadresa, at his shop in Nairobi. The shop was on a very busy road called River Road in the city. It was arranged so that he would sleep in the shop at night, and a 'visi' was arranged for his meals. There was a man who collected laundry every Saturday. The amount received from his dad for all his expenses, including school fees, was one hundred shillings a month. (His older brother under the same circumstances was receiving 150 shs. a month). Unfortunately, the shop stayed open till about ten at night, so he could not go to sleep till after that time. Not only that, but he had nowhere to go until the time when the doors to the shop were closed. All the mattresses were stocked up behind a tall display cabinet in the daytime. After the shop was closed, the bedding came out. Govind's uncle, who was a teacher, got to sleep on another display case, which was nice and wide. Another uncle slept on the floor, while Govind got to sleep on a narrow bench. The bench was a little more than twelve inches wide. It was a little tricky to go to sleep on it. For his pillow, he would use his uncle's cushion that he used to sit on while sewing. It sure made his head itchy all night (a transfer of uncle's itchy bottom!). He also had a bicycle, as school was quite far, and he used it to cycle there and back every day. He came across another student called Harishanker who had a van and he was nice enough to take many a student to school and back in it. He was befriended by Govind, and he agreed to transport him to school and back also, along with others. The arrangement worked out quite well for him. Years passed and he had passing grades at school. Once his uncle informed him that lodging had become available at his house, hence Govind went to stay in his house. Surprise, surprise, Govind came first in his class after staying at his house in about three months! His head teacher, a Mr. Fernandez was as surprised as he was. For the next term he was put in the 'A' class. Unfortunately, that did not last long, as he had to go and live in town once again and subsequently and not surprisingly his marks also deteriorated.

CHAPTER 14

Battle of the Stool

It was a rather interesting state of affairs when Govind was living at his uncle's house. His uncle's younger brother, Bhikhu, also lived with them. Bhikhu was a year ahead of him at school. In his uncle's house, there was only one table, and only one stool. The one who got home earlier occupied the stool immediately and possessed it for all the daylight hours, thereby he got to do his day's studies. The other person that arrived later had nowhere to sit for the day and do his homework! As soon as school was over, the two would rush home with all speed to occupy the stool. The one who did not get the stool did not do his homework that day! What a life!

CHAPTER 15

The Rift Valley

The Rift Valley is very important in the geography of Kenya and forms a part of our story. A brief description follows.

It is a valley that is even longer than The Great Wall of China. It is about three thousand miles long, extending from Syria, Lebanon, Jordan Valley, Gulf of Aqaba, Red Sea, Gulf of Aden, into the Indian Ocean; but the main branch goes south west into the Red Sea, Ethiopia, Kenya, Tanzania, Zambezi River Valley ending up in Mozambique. It started about 50 Million years ago, and is apparently related to the science of plate tectonics. The massive plates started to tear apart slowly, forming the valleys. Its depth varies, from 1296 Feet below sea level at the shores of the Dead Sea, while it is over 6000 feet above sea level in the cliffs of Kenya. Its width can vary from a few miles to over a hundred miles! Many of the depressions in the geologic formation have formed lakes, such as Lake Tanganyika, Kivu, Albert (Mobutu), etc. Some of the areas of the Savannah that is part of the Rift Valley have very rich and varied wild life.

The Denakil Basin in Ethiopia is part of the rift valley. The base of it is 130 meters below sea level. It is one of the hottest regions in the world. Rock salt is mined and transported by camels to other areas of Africa. The Danakil Alps separates the desert from the Red Sea. It is sometimes referred to as 'The roof of Africa'.

CHAPTER 16

❮ ౨୦౪ ❯

Lalji Ramji Gohill

Lalji was a student that hailed from a town called Nakuru, which is a booming town in the Rift Valley about a hundred miles north west of Nairobi. It is famous for the two lakes nearby—the closest one being Lake Nakuru, and the other one is Lake Naivasha. They are famous for their unique wildlife, particularly the flamingos. People from all over the world come to see the awesome sight, especially when these magnificent birds take off on their flight, or come in to land on the lake. It is a sight that once seen is never forgotten.

Lalji along with Govind had a lot of friends that were Ismailis. They were bright students, but appeared to be running a secret society. They had a newsletter that circulated among their friends who were also of the same sect. It was circulated only to other Ismailis and not to be read by anyone else!

Ismailis are Shia Muslims, a branch of Islam that is widespread throughout the world. It would seem that they have a king without a kingdom. They are the followers of the Aga Khan, who lives in Paris with his family, and is head of the sect. He is their religious leader or Imam. They are in over twenty-five countries of the world and include Syria, India, East Africa, England, and Canada and many other countries. In Islam, it would appear that a split occurred over the recognition of the seventh Imam called Ismail. In the ninth century, an Ismaili Dynasty known as the Fatimids ruled as Caliphs in Egypt. The Ismaili Sect is divided into the Misaris and the Mustafians, with the Aga Khan being a leader of the former. They also believe that there are two Imams, the visible and the hidden. The latter, it is believed will appear in the future. The Ismailis have a remarkable cohesiveness, and any small town that has two or more families of the sect has a 'gymkhana', where they gather, give out food to their poor brethren, and often give out loans at a cheap rate, and enquire about the welfare of all the members.

The Aga Khan leads many charity organizations, and the help they give to the poor all over the world is remarkable. In India, a large number of the 'Lohana' caste had changed into Ismailis. It is said that the Aga Kan cannot marry in their system, and has to marry an outsider, hence Rita Haworth and others. Whenever he visits another city, sometimes arrangements are made so that many can get married and blessed by him. All he does is to join the hands of the couples that are getting married.

Lalji was a very meticulous and keen student. He was handsome in its own way, with rather thickset strong musculature, emanating a simian like strength in his hands, heavy jawed, short, with thickset eyebrows that came forwards and upwards like multiple whiskers. He was not very tall, with short, stubby but powerful arms. He dressed immaculately, and did his studies and homework conscientiously and thoroughly. His writing was like pearls. He was also keen to sell subscriptions to Reader's Digest to anyone who would care to buy it. He had a sophisticated and somewhat superior stance, and would rather watch American movies while all is friends watched Indian movies, which were rather inferior and mundane, according to him. His residence was behind where Govind lived, where there was a courtyard, with rooms, kitchens, toilets, and bedrooms upstairs. He lived with his uncle's family and was lucky enough to sleep in the kitchen, where he could go to bed even at 7 p.m., a luxury according to Govind.

He would often get up at six in the morning, and gather a small crowd of friends, then along with the gang go running through the streets of Nairobi. The routine was in fact good daily exercise. He was a good runner and was often at the front of the group, while at the end could be seen Govind struggling along and making heavy work of it all!

The business in Nakuru was run by his father, and it was quite prosperous. It was called Gohill Cycle Mart.

The years in Nairobi stretched from 1943 to 1948. Govind had passing grades, almost never (except once) reaching the 'A' class, which was reserved for the cleverest of the boys, but stayed somewhere in the B, C, or D Classes. As the final years approached, Govind realized that he had no hope at all of passing the forthcoming examination of London Matriculation and Cambridge School Certificate. He had heard of boarding available for students at the 'Shradhanand Brahmcharya Ashram', for accommodation only. It was located out in the country, in an area of Nairobi called The Parklands. He applied and was accepted. During the summer he did not go home, but stayed alone in the place. He studied very hard, day and night. The occasional breaks came when he played the flute, which he played obsessively and rather monotonously.

It happened during one of the semesters. Govind was studying late one night. Each student had a light above his head hanging with an electric wire from the ceiling. So as not to disturb anyone, he had wrapped a damp towel around the light, thereby making sure that only a narrow beam would fall on his work. His concentration was broken after a couple of hours when he smelt smoke. Looking up, he saw the source of the smoke—the towel had caught fire! He removed the towel hastily, and ran out with it. He threw it out into the front courtyard, and thanked his lucky stars that the boarding house had not caught fire!

Lalji, at he same time moved his residence to one of his other uncle's house that was nearby, it being in the Parklands. The two continued their friendship. They decided that they needed extra tutorials in English, and enlisted for evening classes with a teacher called Mr. Noronha. Unfortunately, the said gentleman lived in an area of Nairobi called Eastleigh. To get to his house, the two had to cycle at night through the City Park, an adventure by itself. However, they learnt a lot from the brilliant teacher, and came to no harm despite cycling through the hair-raising park, as it was not safe to go through it even in the daytime. (Mr. Noronha was murdered in the streets of Nairobi some years later).

One day, Mr. Noronha gave an assignment to his students—they were to write an essay on 'The saddest day of your life'. Govind got down to it, and made up a story that as he was sitting in the boarding house alone, he received a telegram that said to the effect that his mother had died. His world was devastated, according to the story. It was full of pathos, and all the students felt sad when Govind read it loud in the class, which he was asked to do. It brought out a tear in the eyes of many of the listeners. Mr. Noronha expressed sadness and expressed and hoped that it was not true. However, the same question was asked in the examination for 'Senior Cambridge', and you would be right in thinking that all of the students wrote the same story as they had already heard it from one individual. Must have been quite an eye opener for the examiner!

He was also an outstanding member of the debating society. At that time there was a controversy raging as to whether the school, which was called Govt. Indian High School, should change its name to 'Duke of Gloucester School' and he took part in the said debate, rather vociferously. He argued against amalgamation but was the outcome was fruitless. The change in the name came about and the Duke himself was present at the renaming ceremonies.

Govind, along with many of his friends, passed the examinations Cambridge School Certificate and London Matriculation, and the high school was over soon afterwards.

CHAPTER 17

Ramayana

During the school breaks when he went to Nyeri for a few days, and continuing even after he left school, he became close to his mother—Zaverben. The closeness with his mother was because of the great book that was called the Ramayana. It is a book of epic proportions, and depicts the life of Rama, who was said to be a manifestation of Vishnu, God incarnate. Vishnu is said to come down in different forms and show mankind the way when he is lost and is steeped in sin. It is one of the main books that all Hindus read. Unfortunately, the book is full of pathos, and the two ended up crying buckets of tears long before the reading was done for the day. In fact, the reading was never completed! It happened every time they opened the great book and made a start. The chapters were not read full, and often the reading had to be abandoned.

CHAPTER 18

❮ ৯o৶ ❯

Hindu Mythology

The Upanishads are the accumulated knowledge of ancient Hinduism. However, every Hindu child is taught the great epics of Hinduism. These epics, along with the Upanishads, are written in the major works called the Ramayana, the Mahabharata and The Gita. Ramayana is written by two great sages of India called Guru Valmiki, and Guru Vishvamitra. The Gita is the preaching of Lord Krishna to Arjun, at his time of crisis. The events that lead them to write the great epics make themselves a worthwhile tale.

The first one is that of Valmiki who was a robber in his earlier years. He wandered in the forest and accosted any traveler that would be in that region, and rob them of their possessions. One day Narad (who is a known troublemaker) came to the area. Valmiki saw him and threatened him and told him to surrender his valuables. Narad said that he would gladly do that, but had a question to ask before he did it. Valmiki agreed to answer his question. Narad asked 'With all the loot you gather, you obviously commit sin. Your family, who partake of your loot, do they also partake of your sins?' Valmiki said that of course they did. Narad said that he was not so sure, so Valmiki tied him to a tree, and went home and asked the same question of the family. The reply was that though the family enjoyed his acquisitions, they would not partake of his sins. This cured him of his delusions. He returned to the forest and released Narad, and settled down to write the epic and became a saint.

The other story is that of Vishvamitra. The latter had married recently, and his wife had returned to her parents. Unable to withstand the separation, he walked to his wife's village through a blinding storm, and on reaching her house, he noted that she was living on the second floor of the house. He gathered a 'chanan gho', a snakelike creature that can act like a rope, and tied it to one end of a rope. Apparently the creature acts like a hook, and holds on to the balcony rather tight, and one can then climb up on the rope. He threw up one end of the rope to the deck above, and then he just climbed up. His wife was amazed to see him and said; 'You risked your life to come and see me through this heavy storm because of your love for me!' If you had such love for God, then you would have no fear not only in this life, but also of the next one. He left immediately, and at these words of wisdom, he decided that he would devote his life to Rama, and wrote the book.

CHAPTER 19

❮❀0❀❯

Govind returns to Nyeri on completing school

Govind completed his studies, and went back home to Nyeri, where he joined his father in business. For some months he worked there conscientiously, but could never care for the way any business is run. He had kept in touch with Lalji, who informed him that he was planning to go to India in three months for further studies. Govind approached his dad who was generally in agreement with Govind's request that he should be given permission to join Lalji to follow further studies in India. In those days choices for education for boys was limited. While the daughters were expected to get married and settle down, the boys went on to study to become either doctors, or engineers or lawyers. He agreed eventually and told him that he could proceed to go overseas and study medicine. Nanjibhai ordered his staff to sew new clothes for his son. The result was unwearable baggy pants, shirts etc. Unfortunately, he would settle down with Govind and a friend of his called Mr. Gajri in many evenings, and lament over the costs involved in his son's venture. Mr. Gajri added fuel to the fire. He pontificated and announced that in his estimates that his friend's son had cost a lot of money in Nairobi, and would even be more so in India, and that also without being in the least accountable. He also thought that the man's son was a blackguard and dishonest. The two commiserated on each other's shoulder, rather unbecomingly.

The next step that was necessary was that of obtaining a passport. A minister of the church, or a doctor was required to sign the forms. Govind knew a Dr. Craig who was working in the Provincial General Hospital in Nyeri, the gentleman having taught him First Aid some months previously in the school in Nairobi where Govind was a student learning first aid under him. He went to see the doctor at the hospital, and presented the forms to him. Dr. Craig's eyes bulged, and he seemed as though he was on fire and burning all over. He stared at the document and hurled it across the table, and told Govind that he was not familiar with him and had no idea as to who he was, and therefore he could not sign the form. Govind was crestfallen and so was his father when he went home and told him what had happened.

Days passed, with father and son crestfallen and at a loss as to how to proceed and get the necessary forms completed so that the young man could get a passport.

One sunny afternoon a gentleman was window shopping by the store. He was an impressive Englishman, with graying hair on the head, cleanly shaven and appeared very upright with a pipe in his mouth. He wore a nice Harris Tweed jacket, with patches at the elbows, and khaki pants. He also mumbled in his speech, making it hard to follow him. The mumbling was worse for the fact that he kept his pipe in his mouth as he spoke. He saw Nanjibhai crestfallen, and asked him what the problem was. Nanjibhai just poured out his problems, and his son's inability to obtain a passport. He thought the whole problem was rather trivial and told Nanjibhai to ask his son to present himself at his office on the next day.

He was in fact the manager of Standard Bank of South Africa in Nyeri. (the gentleman's name was Mr. Weber). Govind presented himself at the appointed time on the next day, and, after asking him a few pertinent questions, he signed the forms without any hesitation whatsoever. Father and son both breathed a sigh of relief. They could not express their deep gratitude and thanks to him. He obviously showed humanity in him.

Govind and Lalji booked to travel to the great country of India on a ship called the S.S.Kampala. Neither had made any arrangements to obtain admission at any of the colleges in India.

INDIA

CHAPTER 20

◀ ৩০৫ ▶

INDIA

Further studies in India

The day finally arrived. Early one morning on a bright sunny day, Govind, with his dad and uncle—Keshavjibhai, left in his dad's Mercedes Benz 220 to go to Kiganjo, the railway station about eight miles away. The road winds through hills and valleys. It had rained heavily the night before and the road was treacherous and very muddy. The car slipped all over the place in all that wet dirt. Quite often his uncle would have to get out and push the car. The station was eventually reached. He bought a ticket to go to Mombasa. The train goes via Nairobi. In Mombasa he met up with Lalji, and they proceeded to the ship that was called the S.S.Kampala. The whole area at the port was a mass of hustle and bustle. There were a large number of passengers on the ship, in the First, Second and Third Class; and of course there were many more on the docks—people who had come to say goodbye to their venturesome youngsters and other relatives who were departing for India. All the passengers were waving, and not to be outdone, Govind and Lalji started to wave, but at nobody in particular, as they had no one to wave to!

The next morning in the early hours, the ship gave out a loud whistle, and made preparations to depart from the docks. The ship left soon for an unknown world. Lalji and Govind along with many others were in the Third Class on the ship. The residence was on an open deck. Mattresses were spread out and one had nothing to do but settle on them and pass the days away. In one corner was a man on a small bed, coughing away day and night. He was dying from Tuberculosis and had elected to return to India, his beloved motherland where he wanted to have his last breath. It started to rain heavily as night approached. Govind and his friend met with some sailors and demanded a cover over their heads. The sailors fixed some tarpaulin so the rain would not fall directly on them. It brought some comfort for them.

Many more of their friends were in Second Class, and the two would go and see them daily. There was a connecting door through which one went to the

'Upper' Class. They would stay in the lounge all day, meet with all and have some drinks and even indulge in some frolic. In the evening they would sneak back quietly into the Third Class to go to sleep.

One day it was announced that all passports were to be surrendered for immigration purposes. When the collectors came, Lalji was having a snooze, and had a towel over his face so no one would recognize him, as obviously he did not care to be noticed that he was in the Third Class.

'Hey Govinda', says he, 'look inside my clothing, you will find my passport there, give it to the collectors.' Govind felt subdued and did it obediently.

The Captain of the ship had suspicions as to what kind of hanky-panky was going on with the passengers on the ship. He had the connecting door closed, as well as have all the bathrooms locked, and then all the passports were returned to their respective owners. Many in the third class did not get their passports, as they were not there when the passports were returned. They were enjoying life with their friends in the Second Class! It turned out to be quite embarrassing, as the Captain had to be seen for a return of the passports. Along with a return of the documents a stiff lecture was forthcoming, admonishing that with such outrageous and dishonest behavior their admission to various colleges in India was threatened. After the strict lecture the passports were returned and the victims made a hasty retreat!

CHAPTER 21

⟨ ✧୦୰ ⟩

Bombay (Mumbai)

The glow of city of Bombay, (Mumbai) early in the morning has to be seen to be believed. It envelops the whole city, and is bright orange in color. Initially it is all-quiet in the morning, but slowly the giant awakens, with unbelievable din and smell that strike the senses. The noise is that of people, bicycle rings, hooting cars, people advertising their wares, including foods and ice cream, while the smell is a mixture of curries, human sweat and discharges, animal excreta, filthy green seawater etc. It appears that the action of all the people vibrate with energy and a rhythm of their own making. It is like a colony of ants. One cannot help but be impressed and overwhelmed by it.

Activities of all kinds start as soon as the big liner comes into harbor, and the gangway is put in place. There are all kinds of signs, specially the ones that say that the Government pays the porters and no payments are to be made by the arriving passengers to them. Every one of the disembarking passengers has one article of bedding, a large metal trunk, and one or two other bags. The bags are quite large, and appear to be in tatters and are overstuffed, with the owners having had trouble closing them as would appear as a strap is placed tightly around it. Even the strap appears in discomfort, and is about to give up the ghost. Porters are dressed in red shirts, a dhoti, and often a turban that was white at one time, and a brass metal identifier that the name is a porter around the left upper arm. The identifier number is engraved in the brass band. They look at the luggage and quote a price for carrying it out of the boat. Then the haggling starts. The porters would start to beg, howl, cajole and scream about anything else that would rouse the pity of the passengers. They even cry and get down on their knees, recalling all the Gods and Goddesses that come to their minds and tongues, and anything else that would arouse sympathy from the travelers. Then the stuff is taken out to the customs shed to be identified and cleared by custom's officers. Eventually the price is agreed upon by all the parties. Customs officers are greedy for a bribe, and when all that is over, and the officer's greed is fed and satiated, then they just throw the open containers on the other side, to be collected by the harassed passengers. Later on, the heat of the day is intense and overpowering, and sweat pours out of every pore of all the living beings, adding to the stink that screams out that it is 'Bombay'.

Laljibhai, who became a chemist in later life and an alcoholic much later, came to collect the duo. He rented a tonga and the entire luggage was loaded onto the tonga, and a ride was taken through the streets of Bombay. (A tonga is a horse drawn carriage). The tonga was driven to a 'Dharmshala', a kind of poorhouse or sanctuary where you live for free. It is run through donations of generous people. He deposited the two along with their luggage in the sleeping area of the dharamshala. The area in fact was a corridor. From there, one could see a lineup of people (which were mostly tattered and malnourished human bodies), waiting to have a shower at the trickling pump present at the head of the queue. The scene was pathetic. The duo refused to stay there. It was getting late in the afternoon, and it was decided that Govind would go and look for accommodation while Lalji would look after all the luggage. As Govind was walking along the main street, a man approached him and asked him for directions to a particular place. The man would not accept the fact that Govind had no idea as to where the place was! He told Govind to wait while he asked for the directions from other people. He would not take a no for an answer, and would not listen to Govind and accept the fact that the new immigrant who had just arrived was in a hurry. He started to give Govind a lecture informing him how rude the young men of today are, etc., but Govind just left him rather abruptly as he had other urgent matters to attend to. He found accommodation at Khetwadi Lane, which was off Sandhurst Road, the main road that leads to Chowpaty, where all Mumbai descends for the night, as it is by the sea. The two had to share a room with two other fine gentlemen, a Mr. Vaidyanath, and Mr. Nayer. The two men were very bright, and very vociferous in politics. In fact if anyone wants to talk politics, they should go to India, a place where the people have verbal diarrhea while discussing politics and everyone has a firm opinion on every subject.

It was interesting to live there, and no matter how hard anyone tried, the people could not pry from the two as to what caste they were, so they just called them 'nanabhai' and 'motabhai', in other words younger and older brother. The nutritional value of the food given was poor, though they had multitudes of pickles with their chapattis. The health of the two suffered as a consequence.

◄࿐0࿐►

CHAPTER 22

❮ ❧0❧ ❯

Saint Xavier's College

Mr. Noronha, the teacher in Nairobi had a brother in India called Father Alphonso, who was secretary to the venerable institution called St. Xavier's College. The two approached him, and gave him about the news of Kenya, and after giving him some presents, expressed the wish to study at the college. He used his influence with higher authorities, with the result that they were accepted in the college. They were to start the 'First Year Science' course.

Nanjibhai was told at one time that sugar was in very short supply in India, so he sent some sugar to India with his son. Unfortunately, there would be customs tax on it, so he heated a mixture of sugar, dye and water, then dried the above syrup, and packed it in a large can or 'dubba'. Govind gave it to Fr. Alphonso as a present, who, though he appreciated it, had no idea as to what it was and what to do with it. In fact the mixture was discarded eventually.

The other stuff that the two were getting regularly from Kenya was cans of butter, and bacon. The two had no idea what bacon was, so they kept the butter for their own consumption, and gave the bacon to Fr. Alphonso. Fr. Alphonso had become quite eager to obtain the cans of bacon, more so than the two looked forward to getting the butter!

Classes began in earnest. There were three groups, each one with 150 students. There were nine subjects to be learnt thoroughly, and they were English, Math, Geometry, Science, Moral Science, and Biology, etc. Indian students make very good and conscientious students, and they are excellent at cramming. Unfortunately, if the results were not favorable, then they would commit suicide on the spot by jumping off the high tower called the Rajabai Tower where results were posted.

It was announced that students could join the National Cadet Corp. or NCC for short. They could join one of three arms of the service, i.e. the army, air corp., or infantry. There were interviews, and it was Lalji who went first, and was immediately accepted into the army, mainly on being asked as to why he wanted to join the army, he said 'I want to serve my country, sir'. Govind gave the same reply and was immediately accepted.

Next came medical examinations. In this the candidate had to take down their pants, and had to jump up and down, while the examiner looked at the testicles, and checked if there was a hernia present. It was odd that this was the complete examination. The health of the heart and lungs was never checked.

Parades started in earnest. The leaders were ignorant of English, and 'attacha' was meant to be attention, and 'standtease' was stand at ease. The guns to be trained on were 25pounders, presumably the weight of the bombs. There was a payment for each participant of the parade, but in fact the money was never handed out.

Marching with Lalji was always hilarious and hazardous. He could not march in synchronicity with others as a consequence of which he was always kicking somebody marching in front or behind him.

'One, two' cried the soldiers alternately', but at the time when it should reach in 'one' ended in 'two'. The sergeant was puzzled, and had the soldiers repeat it a few times. He was eventually able to figure out the problem soldier. It was Lalji, crying out one and two at the same time. 'Kya shadi suda hey'—in other words, are you married and speaking for your wife as well! It was hilarious.

It was a time when India was blessed with politicians of an extremely high caliber. There were Mahatma Gandhi, Jawaharlal Nehru, Vallabhbhai Patel, Subashchandra Bose, Sarojini Naidu (the 'nightingale' of India) as well as many others. It was Mr. Patel who brought India under one rule—he had given an ultimatum to all the rulers (who were the Maharajas, of each state) of India, telling them to join the new union or else. However, to be fair, he made them the Governors of their Provinces. He died some years later, and India gave her hero a massive sendoff.

CHAPTER 23

Preparations to Leave India

Once again the two were getting restless and eager to travel and see other lands. Education in India was good, but the two East Africans were somehow feeling intimidated. Many students in India had the impression that in Africa people lived on trees and were quite backward. It did not help. It also appeared that if you were an East African, the place to enroll was at Wilson's College, which was on a section of Marine Drive, so called the 'Queen's Necklace'. The health of the two was suffering because of the intolerable heat, the poor environment and poor nutrition. Lalji had his father's go ahead and proceed to the great country called England, and he wondered if Govind would like to join him. After some correspondence with his father, Govind's father eventually relented and told him that he could go to England with his blessings. He also sent money for the journey. The two booked to go to England on the MS Batory, a Polish Liner, which was to set sail in about a week's time for England and beyond.

❮❧o❧❯

Ranava revisited

(A place of Filth and Poverty but people with a heart of Gold)

Guilty conscience pricked at the minds of the two, as, even though their relatives were not far off in Gujarat, the two had made no effort to go and see them. The two decided to make a dash for it, and as it was not possible fly to Porbander, Gujarat, the closest city to their grandparent's village, the two decided to go by train, and meet with all the aunts, uncles, grandparents, etc. To go by train would appear to be a stupid mistake as it would be difficult to get back in time and board the ship. The two had booked to go via the Inter Class on the ship. (The trains in India have First Class, Second Class, Air Conditioned Chair Cars, Inter Class and Third Class). (Someone had asked Gandhi at one time why he always went by Third Class; his reply was that because there was no Fourth class!).

'Sir, can I find a place for you two in the train? It will cost you 50 Rupees', said a man to the two at the Railway Station. It was agreed upon, so he grabbed the luggage of the two innocent travelers, and found a compartment that was full of people, and saw some room at one corner. He flung the luggage into that corner and informed the two that he had found the place for them. He was told that that was not satisfactory, and the two went back and changed their tickets for Second Class travel. The man persisted, and kept cornering Govind who was the softer of the two, while Lalji looked in the distance and quietly but firmly mentioned Police, at which the man was like a rag doll and relented, and was happy with a couple of rupees.

Govind was met in Ranavav by his grandfather, Mr. Meghjibhai, and his daughter—Bhanumati. Lalji went with his grandparents. They went home by Rickshaw, with the horse merrily jingling as it trotted along.

The family was so happy to see Govind that Grandma made the special stuff called Lapsi, which is a sweet dish, made with flour, sugar, cooking oil etc., and fed him, and continued to feed him despite objections, till Govind could not consume anymore.

One of grandpa's daughters, called Kadvi who would be Govind's aunt, came over late in the afternoon. As soon as she saw Govind, she started to cry. She cried, and she cried. She cried buckets of tears. She cried all evening, despite being told that time was limited, and Govind was to leave early in the morning. She just could not help herself, and cried incessantly all day, which left no time to socialize with her at all. She was crying when Govind left the village.

Govind was given a container made of brass, with water and 'dahi' (yogurt) in it, which he immediately started to drink. Bhanu, the little girl that was his aunt, pointed it out to the people present, and only then was Govind informed that the mixture was to be thrown on the roof so that the plentiful crows on the roof would have a drink. It was apparently for the benefit of the departed ancestors. Grandpa was quite gracious about Govind's mistake, and the glass was refilled for the necessary purpose.

Govind went to see Radhaben, grandpa's other daughter who lived some distance away, and with whom he had fallen out. He had some tea with her and the family. He gave the children five Rupees each on leaving and on return he told grandpa what he had done. This made them quite unhappy, which was sad in a way.

The next day they took the train again, which was to travel to Jamnagar, and change there to for Rajkot, and eventually to reach Bombay. On the train before Jamnagar, Govind vomited copiously and brought out all that 'lapsi'. He was rather lucky that they had to change the train at Jamnagar as the stink was awful.

The two just stared at their beloved land out of the window of the train that was to Bombay via Rajkot, engrossed in their own thoughts that they would never see the beloved land again. They were emotionally charged and almost on the point of tears.

In the same compartment was sitting a kind gentleman who asked the two if all was well, as they were both looking sad. The two just opened their hearts out and told him about the fact that they were not only saying goodbye to the beloved land, but informed him also of the dilemma of not being able to reach the ship on time. The man was a lawyer, and had just won a case in Cutch, and was on his way home. He told the two that if they got off the train at Rajkot, the town where he was disembarking, he would personally see that the two got an airline ticket to fly to Bombay as he had some influence with the airline there. They all got off at the Station, but his residence was about a mile away from the station. There was a line of rickshaws outside, but as he would not pay the regulation rates as laid down by the government, so they had no choice but to walk all the way, carrying the heavy luggage in their hands. On reaching his house, he just excused himself, and went in to sleep, leaving the two outside, but true to his word, early in the morning he obtained the much-desired tickets, and the two flew to Bombay. The two also breathed a sigh of relief. Boarding the ship now appeared possible.

ENGLAND

CHAPTER 25

◀ ℘o℘ ▶

ENGLAND

London

The destination of the ship that was called the M.S.Batory, was Gdynia, Poland. It was to sail via the Suez Canal, stopping at Alexandria, Gibraltar, and making a short stop at Southampton in England. All the passengers for England disembarked at Southampton. One had to catch a train to London from the port of Southampton. The ship then proceeded to the city of Gdynia.

It was the first time the two had met Polish people. They impressed them with their handsome appearances, their extremely good food, and extreme politeness.

On the ship a Mr. Thorn befriended the two. He was Anglo-Indian, and had never before left the shores of India. He was well dressed, but very anxious and a hesitant man. He explained to them that it was the first time he had left India and was worried. He said he would be very grateful if the two would look after him. The two agreed, which was a bit silly as they themselves were novices and inexperienced in world travel and humanity in general. How indeed can they care for anyone?

They were vegetarians (not even eating eggs or fish), and the sight of people sitting on proper tables and being served filled them with awe and admiration (as they had glimpsed on the ship in second class that was taking them to India from Kenya on the S.S. Kampala. It was the time on the ship when they were visiting their friends in the highbrow or snooty class, as they felt).

The ship reached Alexandria about 2 a.m., and anchored for about three hours. Many shops were open for the convenience of the visitors. There was a vendor who on bare feet, selling a lot of bric-a-bracs—all the articles on a small makeshift wooden platform on his tummy. It was tied to his neck with a strap. Mr. Thorn showed some interest in an article, which can be attached to the lapel of a jacket, but decided not to buy it. The Vendor followed him wherever he went. At one point he offered it for free, and put it on his lapel. Then he demanded money—Mr. Thorn was to pay any money that his heart wished. Again Mr. Thorn refused, and the haggling started. The vendor was on the point of pulling out his knife, but fortunately it was time to board the ship and cast anchor—what a relief!

The next port was Aden where the two got a little anxious, as even accommodation in England was not booked. The two wrote a letter hastily to the British Council in London, requesting them if they can arrange for the two to stay on arrival. After passing the rock of Gibraltar, and the stormy sea of the Bay of Biscay, the shore of the majestic British Isles was seen. Many, along with the two, disembarked at Southampton, and took the train to London. On arrival in London, the two were told that boarding was arranged at a house owned by a Mr. and Mrs. Jason living in Bounds Green. Staying there worked out quite well, but it was felt that they were being overcharged. Later, the two found a place where boarders were taken, and that was at King's Cross.

CHAPTER 26

King's Cross or Saint Pancras

The place is so called because of the statue of King George the IV was erected here, but was taken down after ten years. It is also the place where there is the entrance to the 'chunnel' where the trains travel to and from France under the sea. The railway station is rather huge. Grays Inn is also nearby where a large number of trainees go to study law and become 'Barristers'

The two saw an advertisement that boarding was available at one of the hotels in King's Cross. A visit there was generally satisfactory, and it was decided to move there. The two were shown a small room with a double bed and a fireplace. They were assured that the double bed would be removed and two single beds would be placed there—something that never happened.

One evening, Govind was feeling energetic, and remembering his days at the NCC, put on his army boots, and started to march. One two, one two, up and down the room he marched, with precision and gusto. He hit the fireplace with his boots by accident, and there were pieces of the fireplace flying all over the place. These were upright pieces of clay, into which the gas burns and gives out heat. The two went out in search all over town to buy these clay replacements before the landlady finds out and boots them out of the place. Luckily, they were able to get it, and a relief it was too! However, it was impossible for the two to lie in the same bed, as continuous scratching, turning, snoring of each one got on the nerves of another. They longed to sleep separately. They looked around for accommodation again, and found lodgings at Primrose Hill Road.

CHAPTER 27

❦

1-3 Primrose Hill Road

Accommodation at Primrose Hill Road was quite satisfactory and the two made some progress in their education also. A Mr. and Mrs. Heatley owned the boarding house. Mr. Heatley was a bright and a well educated man. He appeared to be a deep thinker. He was able to name any day in any year given the date. He gave the formula to Govind, and it worked well. Mrs. Heatley was a heavyset buxom lady. She had a good heart, and really cared for all the persons in residence. Primrose Hill itself was behind the house, and was a good place for meeting people. One took the bus to the college, by crossing over the hill and walking towards Baker Street, or catching the train at Chalk Hill. The next station on the route was Camden Hill, the place where Charles Dickens, the great author lived. Baker Street of course is famous for 'Sherlock Holmes'. He is said to have his offices in Baker Street, but in truth no such person as Sherlock Holmes ever existed. He was Sir Arthur Conan Doyle's fictional character.

The rooms were rather large, and the two shared their room with a black gentleman called Mr. Awori. Mr. Awori was from Uganda and was an Engineering student. He got up at six every morning, bright and early and started to brush his hair in an effort to remove all the curves and crinkles out of his Negroid hair. Brush, brush, brush, he went on and on! Swish, swish, swish the annoying sound went. No one told him that it was impossible to uncurl his hair in that way as nature did not intend it to be straight. It was frustrating for him and even more so to the sufferers in the room. The two could not sleep at that hour, and once after a hasty meeting, they decided that Mr. Awori was to be approached and told to leave and go to a different room. He had ignored previous requests to desist the procedure. Requests for him to stop the habit had fallen on deaf ears. It led to heavy depression in him, and he spent a whole day with a pencil in his hand, and swinging it backwards and forwards, repeatedly, and he kept comparing the swinging of the pencil to the pendulum to life, what with all of its up and down. It was a pathetic and a sad sight but also a little comical.

As the toilet was quite far (it was at the other end of the corridor), Govind invented an ingenious device. There was a sink in the corner, and it was used with the contraption. The contraption was used when it was necessary to empty one's bladder at night. One had to get a chair near the sink, and then stand on it, and use the device, which was a funnel attached to tubing—the other end of which was inserted into the drainage hole in the sink. One could then empty one's bladder to his heart's content into the funnel! What a relief it was too!

At one time Govind had to share his room with a man called Mr. Twentyman, as Lalji was away. He was a thin little man that never said much. He was interesting in that he never, ever, changed his pajamas, or never had them washed. He was quite dirty and had a peculiar and a unique smell about him.

In residence there was also a young man called Cyril, who thought that he was psychic. He would have séances in the evenings, and conversed with spirits. One particular evening, he offered to hypnotize Govind. No matter how hard he tried, Govind could not be hypnotized, but, just to oblige, Govind did some maneuvers that were asked of him, like raising the arm etc., but he could not oblige with many of the other postures that were ordered.

"You know, Cyril", Lalji said in a low whisper, "Govind has trouble understanding English sometimes!" Govind felt like opening his eyes and telling everyone to shut up so he could concentrate on going to sleep and entering a trance like state, if possible!

One of the other residents was Christopher Hannigan or Chris for short. He came from Ireland. A nice quiet, shy man who had an Irish temper! He was too shy to go down for dinner, so one of his friends—Govind or Lalji brought it up to him. He had only one pair of pants, the ones he was wearing. He had a large smelly ammoniac stain in the genital area. At night he would take his pants off and go to sleep. He had a girl friend called Pat (Patricia Morgan) who lived at the other end of the city, an area called Morden, which was at the end of the Northern Line on the 'tube'. The 'tube' is the so-called underground trains in London. She would come to see Chris, and do all his washing, ironing etc, but because of the long ride, she would snooze and missed her station where she was to get off now and then. She was a wonderful sweet natured person, and the four of them spent a lot of time together, especially at the council swimming pools. No wonder the two kept failing their examinations. Often, Pat would buy a ticket to go to the next station from Morden, and meet Chris at the other end, who would have bought two tickets and traveled from one and met Pat at the next station. The two would then travel together, getting of at Chris's station. It was an ingenious devise that saved them a lot of money.

Chris at one time bought a cute little black and white dog and called it 'Butch'. He bought a small basket and put it in the corner of the room. He was good to the dog, except when the dog had an accident, when Chris's Irish temper would really show. He would remove his belt from his waist and give the dog a good thrashing—so much so that the dog could be heard howling even on Primrose Hill.

Chris was a good singer, and entertained everyone with his Irish repertoire. He never worked but disappeared at times. At these times it was thought that he had gone to one of the 'bookie' shops nearby where he bet on horses. He probably lost a lot of money as well.

There was another resident from South Africa who thought he was an opera singer. He asked Lalji quite often to hold a hat in front of his mouth, so that he could see the hat vibrate as he sang. The vibration never happened but it sure made a comical scene, what with a young man holding a hat in front of the mouth of a singer! He was a tenor, and his loud voice was could be heard on Primrose Hill!

The two were sharing a room in the attic at one time in No. 3. There was a connecting door to No. 1. At lunchtime, this door was opened and a connection with an electrical outlet made on this side. The other ends were made raw and inserted in a glass filled with water. An egg was put in the water, and a boiled egg was obtained a few minutes later that made a good part of a delicious lunch. Unfortunately, sometimes the fuse would blow and bedlam begun. The connection was quickly removed, and the light bulb screwed in once again. The door was closed and the two acted innocently. It helped as the fuse blew in No. 1 while they were the residents in No.3, as everyone thought! To change a fuse at that time was quite a job.

One particular day all the four roommates were each in their respective corners. It was a dull, cloudy and a boring evening. There was a light drizzle, and of course no incentive to go outside. Our friend Lalji had a bright idea, and light in his head lit up. He gathered a table and chair; and on the table he put a mirror, and a cloth. He made himself comfortable on the chair. He collected a pair of epilating forceps. As you can guess, he wanted to tackle his nose hair. He looked in the mirror, and then inserted the forceps, and tugged, and pulled out a hair. He gave a sharp jerk and a cry of pain. Even though his eyes watered heavily, he had an expression of delight as he stared at the vibrissa. He felt as though he had accomplished a marvel! He repeated the process time and again. It was painful even to watch him, but one could not help but see him with some fascination and even admiration!

One evening Govind was having a snooze. It was a muggy and a boring evening. All was quiet and it was somewhat of a boring evening. Unbeknown to him, someone came and painted his face with black soot, which is readily available in fireplaces. There was an accident outside on the road, and all ran out to see it, including Govind. On reaching the site, he noticed that the onlookers were keener on watching him rather than the scene of the accident. It was much later that he was informed that his face was a black mess.

CHAPTER 28

❮❧o❧❯

Education

The two registered initially at British Tutorial College at Tottenham Court Road in London. It was a good college, but unfortunately it was a private college and the fees were much higher. The nearby YMCA was a great place to study, as they had good desks and chairs just right for diligent students. It was also a good place for lunch. Mr. Crittendon, a minister who frequented the Y.M.C.A. and who was a missionary overseas at one time, befriended the two. He went for lunch with the two poor students, but never paid, leaving the two unfortunate students to foot the bill! Unbelievable!! He did not realize, but his 'Christianity' was misplaced, and not impressive because of his behavior. At one time, in frustration he shouted out at them, 'Why would the two of you not accept Christ as your savior? He was even your color!'

It was amazing that Govind's dad in Kenya knew about the college. Govind had informed him via a letter, rather proudly, that he was attending the particular college. Called the British Tutorial College at Tottnham Court Road. A curt reply had arrived which told him to leave the college immediately as it was a privately run institution and the fees would be much higher.

There was also another time when he was sitting a little too close to the heater while studying and the bottom of his pants caught fire. The heaters were small and circular giving out concentrated infrared heat. He was able to contain the fire, but it left a big hole in the pants. He wrote to his dad that he needed new pants, as the one he was wearing had a hole in it. He left out the part about the fire. The immediate reply was that Govind was a lazy slob (called 'Labad' in Gujarati) who was sitting near a heater and caused the damage. Instead he should get down to his studies and stop just sitting around in front of heaters!. Amazing! Did he have a sixth sense or something! He wrote once to his dad that it was a cold country, and he needed a coat. Nanjibhai got his tailors busy, and they sewed a coat—a baggy one at that, with a large jutting out bottom at the back. It gave the appearance of a proud peacock! Govind just hated it. He had it dyed in a laundry, but it made no difference to its appearances. He just had to throw it away eventually.

The two enrolled in Battersea Polytechnic, but later on moved to Chelsea Polytechnic, to study 1st MB (Bachelor of Medicine) and also Advanced Levels in Chemistry, Physics and Biology, the subjects being the same for both the 1st MB and the A. Levels. The two were told that they needed to pass 2 of the 3 A. Level subjects. This was to the two guys who were used to studying nine subjects in India! Govind, because of his very hard work, obtained the highest marks in Physics, second highest in Biology, and good marks in Chemistry. In other words, his achievement was the highest of anyone in the class. Lalji at that time had started to have excruciating backaches, and was trailing behind.

At one time Govind had his examinations in a place called Teddington. He looked up the 'underground' map, and worked out that he would have to change the train at Piccadilly Circus, and it was the second station after that. The next day he left bright and early. At one of the stations he asked a man if he was going the right way, heading towards Teddington. The man told him to follow him, as he was also going there. About six stations passed, but no sign for Teddington, so he asked the man again, and the man said that he thought Govind had said Paddington. To confuse it even more, there is also a Ferringdon. After getting off at Teddington, he asked someone for the Examination Hall, and it turned out that it was about half a mile's walk. To save money, he walked all the way without realizing the distance involved—no wonder he was late, and as a consequence his marks were poor.

CHAPTER 29

The Two Novices

The world would appear to be rather strange for someone coming from primitive Africa. While they were studying at Tottenham Court Road, they passed a big restaurant called J.Lyons and company. The food there appeared mouth watering but the two were too shy to go in. Govind eventually overcame the shyness, and ventured inside and had a meal of a lifetime. There was a central area where they were selling candies. He went there and tried to buy some, when he was asked for coupons besides the money. He had no idea what that was, but it was no problem, as good Samaritans were nearby and offered their coupons. There was a time when the two were walking in Leicester Square, when they had a desire to go to the washroom. Govind was done in a few minutes, but not Lalji, who refused to use the urinals, and wanted to go in the toilet to empty his bladder. After finding the necessary change, he opened the door, while the attendant who was nearby noticed that the toilet was out of toilet paper. Once again, there was a wait while he went and got the toilet paper.

The two at one time obtained tickets for a theatre called the Palladium, but they were afraid in case someone they were familiar with noticed them going in, and therefore sneaked in rather quietly into the theatre and saw an extravaganza they would never forget.

During the long vacations Govind used to go to Kenya to visit the family. At these times Lalji could not go to Kenya for some reason or another. In Nakuru, he would see Lalji's beautiful mother, who cried whenever she saw Govind, as she thought that her lost son Lalji had come to visit. She died of breast cancer some years later. He also met the other two of Lalji's sisters, Rama and Sharda. He kept in touch with them both. Rama has immigrated to Calgary, married to a Bank Manager, and has lovely children who are a success in their lines of venture. The other lady resides in England.

CHAPTER 30

❄❧०❧❄

Liverpool in sight

G ovind applied to about sixteen universities for admission to start medical studies and become a doctor. He had two replies, one from St. Bartholomew's College in London, and the other from the University of Liverpool.

The interview at St. Bartholomew's did not go well, but it was not surprising as they were seeking students of the right color.

The next interview was in Liverpool. He took the train to Liverpool. The terminus for the city is at Lime Street Station, which also is the red light district of the famous city. He had to walk up Brownlow Hill, one of the slums of Liverpool to reach the university. He started to wish that he would not gain admission in the university, as the street was dirty and unkempt. His interview was with the Dean—Mr. Jack Legate and other members of the staff. Mr. Legate was a missionary in China at one time. He was tall, thin, with circular glasses. One could see education and humanity emanating from the man. He told Govind that he could get admission into the second year of Medicine, provided the Colonial Office in London gave the necessary recommendation. At that time all students had to go through the Colonial Office, even before they came to the country! They had a standard letter to tell the students to change their minds, and choose alternative pursuits such as dentistry etc. as there was no chance that they would be admitted into any Medical Schools, as the standards of education required in England were very high. Govind phoned them, and told them about the interview he had in Liverpool, and about his own achievements, and requested an interview with them. The Colonial Office realized that in fact there was no need for an interview as Govind's marks were good. However, he was given an interview with a Miss Osborne at the said offices. She told him that Liverpool University had a good name and Govind would be happy there and that the necessary recommendation would be given. He was to start in the second year, and was accepted by Mr. Legate into the University. It was not until six months later that he asked Govind for a proof that he had in fact passed the first year in London. What a trusting gentleman!

CHAPTER 31

❮❦0❧❯

University of Liverpool

Wow, what a university! Govind doubted if there were any finer universities in the world! The university had its compliment of the greatest teachers in the world. Thus the writer of the Textbook in Medicine, Professor Cunningham taught there; so did Professor T.N.A. Jeffcoate, the writer of a book called the Textbook of Gynecology. There were many other names—Professor Sheehan of the famous 'Simmonds-Sheehan Syndrome', Professor Harrison who wrote the Textbook of Human Embryology, but to top them all was Lord Cohen of Birkenhead. His beginnings were rather humble. He lived in a house in Hartington Road. He passed University with flying colors, later becoming a teacher in Medicine, and called Professor Cohen. Later he was knighted, and he was called Professor Sir Henry Cohen. The highest honor was accorded to him by the Queen when he became Lord Cohen of Birkenhead. Whenever he gave a lecture, the hall was full, and often there not evens standing room.

Studies started in earnest. Anatomy was taught by dissection of the human body. Many students could not stand the sight of dead people lying in a row, and because of it, some even quit the idea of studying medicine. There was an examination every six weeks on the part that was dissected. A Professor Gregory taught physiology, and unfortunately some cats, or frogs or other animals were put to sleep, or euthanized, after s study was made of the actions of the heart, etc. Organic Chemistry was studied at the same time. In the later years followed Pathology, Pharmacology, Histology and Histopathology, Clinical studies including Obstetrics, Gynecology, Medicine, Surgery etc. Finals came and Govind passed, obtaining the degrees in Bachelor of Medicine and Bachelor of Surgery—MBBS. London exams for L.R.C.P., M.R.C.S. were tried and he passed Pathology but did not make the grade in clinical medicine. There appeared some prejudice in the examiner's eyes and behavior when he went for this particular examination.

The signature tune of the University was (and was sung to the tune of the 'Grenadier Guards'):

74

**SOME TALK OF DRAIN INSPECTORS AND SOME OF
ENGINEERS
WE WOULD NOT GIVE FOR EITHER, LAST WEEKS
VAGINAL SMEARS
SO ON WE GO MARCHING, THE PRIDE OF ALL THE POOL
JACK LEGATE'S JOY ARE THE STURDY BOYS OF THE
LIVERPOOL MEDICAL SCHOOL**

CHAPTER 32

❮ ❧o❦ ❯

Mobility

One of the problems right at the start was that of mobility as the lectures were given at the university, while the practical aspect of learning was at different hospitals which were scattered all over the city. At times there was not much time between the attendance at one place and then the next. There were some classmates who had cars. Unfortunately they felt very important because they had a car, and were suspicious of anyone who befriended them. There was David Parry who had a Mini Minor, and then there was Mike Eisner. Mike had an old Austin, but the only problem was that the brakes in the car were rather poor. If he ever approached a junction when the traffic lights were red, then there was trouble. He would brake and brake, and make the car go over onto the pavement where it would eventually come to a halt. It was a rather hairy situation! As you can imagine, there were not many that were keen to get a ride from him! Govind solved the difficulty of travel by buying a bicycle and riding it all over the city.

Cycling in Liverpool was quite a challenge. There were many ups and downs. At one time Govind obtained accommodation in Birkenhead, which is across the Mersey River on the other side, in a place called St. Aidan's College. The College was for students in theology, but they also had room for university students. To go to the university from the place of residence, one had to go through the tunnel, or take the ferry on the Mersey River. The tunnel entrance was about a mile away from the residence, so one had to cycle there, then negotiate the tunnel, which is 3 miles long. The ride through the tunnel was downhill for the first section and then started uphill in the later half, and after the exit the road continued uphill until you reached the university. One has to take advantage of the downhill road by gathering enough speed so that the uphill becomes less of a strenuous affair. (Cycling is now forbidden through the Tunnel).

David Parry also lived in the residence at the college. He was tall with freckles galore on his face, handsome, with gingery hair. He was full of his own importance, and looked down on anyone who came from the commonwealth, or even anyone who spoke a different language, or accent, or had a different color. When he was in good mood, especially when he was in the bathroom, he would sing very incoherently but loudly making everyone think that he was singing Indian songs and he made it appear as though the foreign students were without class. He studied very hard, but was unhappy if Govind appeared to know more than he did. He felt really unhappy when Govind beat him at table tennis, the game they played quite often, and unfortunately for him, Govind was the better player. David's mother ran a drugstore in Rhyl, North Wales. Govind had the honor to visit them one day.

❮☙◉❧❯

CHAPTER 33

Saint Aidan

A word about St. Aidan—he was the Irish monk of Iona, Ireland, and was made the Apostle of Northumbria in England in c690. He was the founder of Lindesfarne Monastery, and was known for his personal holiness, eloquent preaching, scholarship, charity, and being a miracle worker. At his death a shaft of light was seen ascending his soul to heaven. He is represented as calming the storm and fire, holding up a lighted torch, with a stag on his feet.

There was no man who was as simple, scholarly, sweet natured and representative of the Saint as the principal of the college as Dr. Scott. He was a wonderful gentleman. Unfortunately, he died of a bleeding duodenal ulcer at a young age. His wife was a buxom lady who loved to cook. She also had made a study of geography and wrote some papers on it.

The food and the fellowship were excellent at the college. The students were all devoted to their calling and must have made great ministers for the church in the future. Govind resided there for some time, and was quite happy there except for the fact that during the holidays the place would empty out, leaving him all alone in a vast college residence. It was a bit scary, so he bought a goldfish, which, believe it or not, gave him a lot of fun. He would watch it for hours, and would even put his hand in the bowl and swirl the water around. It was interesting to see the fish turn around and swim against the current. The Scotts family invited him for his meals, which by the way were excellent. However the distance of travel everyday from St. Aidan's to the university was a little too much to negotiate, so Govind moved once again to a boarding house in Liverpool. It was called Methodist International House or HIM as the matron of the residence, a Mrs. Collinson, used to call it. Mrs. Collinson was a fantastic lady, very devoted and considered all the residents as her flock, or like Christ, lost sheep. She was always well dressed and looked radiant, and often came and sat with the residents in the lounge. The only problem was that her digestion was not good, and she passed wind quietly, unfortunately making the whole room quite malodorous!

Living at the MIH was interesting. There was a lounge, with a fireplace. Govind, as a volunteer, made it a habit of going to the cellar to bring up coal for use in the fireplace so that all would have a cozy fire. He did this every day. One day he did not do it, and all the residents were up in arms and very upset with him! There was a student called Mr. Kwame, who came from Nigeria. One evening he went into the lounge, and told everyone to get up. He then moved the chairs by 90 degrees so that they faced a different direction. It was very odd. Next day he was found in the toilet of Lime Street Station, dead. He had died of a Brain Tumor!

There was also another student from Ghana, who locked himself in his room, and started to scream and wanted to commit suicide—the pressure of work in the Medical School was too much for him. Someone had to get a ladder, and put it on the wall on the outside, and climb up to his room through a window and bring him down. He was soon sent packing home.

Another student there was called Peter Caldwell, who could also not take the pressure, and had started to ramble in the beginning. He said that during the holidays he used to go to Burnley, which was just up north, and visit a pond. When he looked in the water in that particular pond, the fish he knew well used to appear and look at him with its beady eyes and hated him, and he had sworn and even told the fish that one day he was going to catch it. One day he did, so he said. His bombastic tales got worse and eventually he quit medical school, as the pressure was too much for him and he was slowly cracking up.

MIH had many students who had come from Ceylon. They were very clever, and most of them were doctors who had come for further education to the venerable institution. (Liverpool ran a program in M.Ch. Orthopedics in Surgery, for those who already possessed the F.R.C.S., and was world renowned for it). (M.Ch.,Orth. stood for 'Master in Orthopedics, and F.R.C.S. for Fellow of The Royal College of Surgeons). Some had come with their wives, who were bored as their husbands were away for long periods and naturally wanted to be entertained by someone else, in more ways than one, if you catch my drift.

There was a Persian dental student called David Habib. He was a good and hardworking student. At one time he had appendicitis, and had to go to Hospital to have his appendix taken out. He came back to MIH for recuperation. From his room he could look across the corridor, and see another student's room. He saw Daphne, the wife of one of the doctor go to this student's room and spend a lot of time there behind closed doors. There was no doubt that there were shenanigans going on. The good doctor was busy studying in the university at the time.

It was at the time when Govind was living at MIH that his bike was stolen. He also found it hard to study in such a busy and noisy environment and to top it off he had also become a vegetarian. He became a friend to David, and they decided to move out together and live elsewhere. They found accommodations in 31 Botanic Road, which was across the beautiful Botanic Gardens. The accommodation did not include food. There was a kitchen and a bedroom. The bedroom was a good size, but it was in the attic and unfortunately the ceiling was only about 2 Feet above the bed. It was awkward to sleep on the double bed that was there. It was also very cold, and despite using a hot water bottle, it remained cold. So Govind and his friend just took the thick rug that was on the floor and put it on top of the bed. They were a little warmer that way. However, the rug was dusty and dirty. On Sundays they listened to 'Top Twenties', which was broadcast by Radio Luxembourg. They broadcast the best top twenty songs that were on the pop chart for that week.

David's girlfriend was a charming girl called Lilian, and a more charming girl one could not come across. Unfortunately she worked in a town called Southport which was quite a distance away. She had to take the train from Southport after a full day's work, then take a bus at the station in Liverpool, and travel to Botanic Gardens. Then she would cook for the two anxious and permanently hungry mouths. When that was done, and after completing other chores like laundry, cleaning up etc. it was time for her to start her journey back. Even then, there was not a word of discontent from her. David eventually qualified as a dentist and opened about three practices. He employed other dentists and put them to work in these places. There were political troubles in Persia at the time, and this affected his practice. He changed his name to 'David Habib', which before that time was 'David Habibollahi' at the time so as to continue his lucrative practice. He married Lilian after he qualified, and they had two wonderful children. One is a male nurse in Psychiatry, and the other one is a Lawyer.

David liked buying and selling cars, but would rather not pay much for it—and he would haggle and bring the price down. At one time he was to buy a car, and took Govind along. The man selling the car was a Mr. Hardy. As soon as he heard that Govind was a medical student, he requested that Govind follow him to another room. In the other room, he just dropped his pants down. Govind was aghast, as he did not know what it was all about. Mr. Hardy kept saying, 'Look, can't you see how small it is? 'Can you not do something about it?' Govind realized that he was talking about his small penis and promised him that he would look into it, and enquired of his mentor, the consultant surgeon that he was under at the time who suggested that the man's penis could be enlarged with a bone graft. Mr. Hardy was informed of it but he did not like the idea and never undergo the procedure.

While living in Botanic Gardens, Govind bought a motorcycle—a BSA Bantam 125 ccs. It was not very powerful but quite zippy. He had started to drive it although he had no idea how the different controls on it worked. He started the engine, and engaged the gear. The motorbike moved, but he had no idea as to how to stop it, so he dragged his foot on the ground—it was ineffective and hurt a lot. Fortunately he was not going fast and solved the problem by just falling off.

Some months later he even bought a similar motorbike and delivered it to Lalji who was in Birmingham at the time.

He learnt to drive it eventually and enjoyed it. It was remarkable how little gas it consumed. At one time his uncle, who was a teacher, was visiting him. The uncle was to visit various schools in the area as part of his curriculum, as he had also come to learn about the great working of the English school system. Govind was volunteered to drive him to these schools. It was comical, as he was taller and towered over Govind when they were driving. Once it was raining as they were driving along, and the motorcycle wheels got caught in the discarded but still present evil tram rails. These rails were a nightmare to all cyclists and motorcyclists. It was raining and the rails as well as the road were slippery. Anyway, no matter how hard he tried, Govind could not extricate his motorbike from the rails where the wheels were caught, and the two had a disastrous fall. There were two bruised bodies, not only physically but also in their ego.

The owner of the house was a Mrs. Pottage. She was not very tall, green old skirt and separate blouse, with a square face, painted with heavy doses of makeup, and had always a cigarette in her hand or in her mouth. She was edentulous, as she could not put up with her dentures. Her husband was in the navy and came home only occasionally. As a result, she was unhappy, lonely and frustrated, sexually and otherwise.

'What does Govind do in the evenings?' she asked David at one time, being obvious as to what she meant. Govind was too devoted to his studies to pay attention to it.

Govind paid a visit to the town of Morthoe in Devon at one time along with his friend David and his girlfriend Lilian. They went for a swim in the sea close by, and had a photograph taken. She looked gorgeous in her swimsuit, standing next to Govind. Anyway, Govind had the photograph in his pocket when he was visiting Kenya, and Jamnadas, being nosy, found it. He showed it to father and claimed that Govind had a girlfriend in England. Nanjibhai knew what was going on, and told Govind to quietly go into Jamnadas's room at night when he was asleep, find the photograph, and tear it up. That was done.

There was also a time when his younger brother, Maganlal had come to Liverpool, and had started studies in the Faculty of Laws in the University to become a lawyer. The degree he was aiming for and later achieved was Bachelor of Laws, or LLB. On the first day they went by bus to the town, and after reaching the town Govind informed him that he had left his motorbike at the university so they would have to go there and get it. Maganlal was really scared as he imagined a big powerful super duper bike, but was happy when he saw it and thought it appeared harmless. In fact he was quite comfortable riding on it as a passenger afterwards.

CHAPTER 34

❦

Europe

There was a Medical Student called Rodney Harris. He was a brilliant student and had a brain that was like a sponge, not only for its retentive memory, but holding it there and reflecting the 'shine' as and when needed.

He was a year ahead of Govind, but, because of his brilliance, after completing the examination for anatomy and physiology, he was offered a scholarship in research, and on if it was concluded satisfactorily he would be granted a degree of Bachelor of Science or B.Sc. He wrote his research on the chosen subject in a usual and brilliant treatise and published it. It held him back for a year. Often Govind would read up about any particular section of his medical studies, and motorcycle to Rodney's house, and, after greeting his Rodney's wonderful parents, he would see Rodney and ask him questions on what he had just read. It was downright disparaging to hear him—he was better than a textbook! He had piles of textbooks by his chair, thrown on the ground after having read and memorized them.

He also had a motorcycle on which he came to the university. He decided that he would like to go on a motorcycle trip to Europe and started looking for a partner. He advertised it on the notice board in the university. Govind saw it and approached him, and told him that he would be willing to go, but he did not have a driver's license yet. 'No problem', said Rodney, as he said he would drive all the way. Preparations started. He announced that as the two were going, the motorbikes the two had were rather small and therefore inadequate for the journey. He knew a lecturer at the University who had a motorcycle and would give it to the duo for their travel if asked. The motorcycle was a BSA 250ccs. It was in fact a discarded and neglected old wreck lying on the university grounds for some years without it ever being used. So the first step was to get it all fixed up. Check out the engine and make it workable. Replace a worn tire, get the engine tuned, etc. It cost a lot of money even before it was even made roadworthy.

The day for travel arrived, and the two started the journey. It was to go through three countries—France, Germany and Belgium after leaving Britain.

The driver was Rodney all the way. The appearances were rather comic, but also stupid and somewhat dangerous. Behind the driver was Govind. The two were dressed with rather thick sweaters and a long coat, a helmet and big boots. In between them were two suitcases, which of course belonged to the members of the party. In fact Govind had to sit at a distance on the back seat as the middle section was occupied by the luggage. It made the motorcycle rather unsteady. Anyway, the trip was to Dover, and then by means of a ferry to Calais in France.

The white cliffs of Dover are famous. They are white because of all that chalk! And they are over 100 meters tall. After reaching Calais, the two started for Paris. The friendliness of all the drivers was astounding—they appeared to be well behaved, many had their families with them, and waving at one and all as they passed by. The cars were all polished and clean. They looked like expensive cars.

It was raining heavily as they reached Paris, and the slippery cobbled streets made motorcycle driving on them dangerous. The two did not have much money, so they went to hostels, but only after hiding the motorbike or keeping it far off, along with the helmets, so no one suspected them of not being hitchhikers!

The motorcycle turned out to be even more frustrating. Once stopped, it would refuse to start, and Rodney had to run down a hill with it, engage the gear and get it going. It was only possible to stop on top of a hill for pit stops, restaurants, washrooms, etc. Stopping where there was not a downhill was out of the question.

There are no words that can describe Paris, for its sheer beauty, history, layout etc. Add to the great aspect are the Louvre Museum, the Champs-Elysées, the Napoleon Bonaparte Mausoleum, the Bastille, the Eiffel Tower etc. All these in fact take your breath away. Nightlife in Paris is yet another story. However, France was left behind, and Germany was the next country to visit.

On leaving France, the custom's gate was reached at the border. It was opened after proper examinations of all the documents etc. unfortunately it was uphill on leaving and the motorbike could not be started. The officers had to open the gate once again so that the motorbike could be started by running downhill. The gate had to be reopened once again so that the duo could enter Germany again and leave France behind! Soon after entering Germany, Govind started to sing with gusto what he had heard Rodney sing in the past-a song about 'Deutschland Deutschland himayawe', without realizing that it was not a song to be sung. Rodney turned red faced quite often, turned beet red. However, it was too late to realize the mistake.

In Germany the two entered the autobahn. It is a divided highway that is like nowhere else in the world. There is no speed limit, and drivers can go at any speed they choose. As they drove, one of the tires burst. It was surprising that help came along immediately; the efficiency of the Germans has to be seen to be believed. There was a serviceman on a motorcycle who appeared immediately. He assessed the damage, told them that they needed to buy a new tire. He took out his notebook, looked up the prices and quoted the price of a tire and after suitable agreement with the parties concerned, he drove to the next town, brought it back and fixed it on the motorbike in no time. It was nothing short of amazing.

The two were visiting a restaurant at one time. The waiter soon saw that the two did not understand German. Trying to save money, they asked for water. He brought some wine. He was told that the two only wanted water, so he brought mineral water and charged heavily for the whole thing. The water appeared eventually.

They visited different towns like Aachen, Koln, Bonn, Dusseldorf and drove through the Black Forest. Düsseldorf was interesting in that there were tiny rooms built in the railway station. The station was underground, and one could stay overnight in one of these rooms for a nominal charge. Köln cathedral is worth a visit.

The two left Germany and entered Belgium, a rather flat but beautiful land, where tulips, daffodils and other flowers grow in abundance. In Belgium the two visited the capital Brussels, where they had a good time. On leaving Germany, they noticed that they needed gas in the tank of the motorcycle, and it was odd that the change the two had of the currency of the country they left behind was exactly right for a fill up of petroleum in the motorbike. Up to today, it is not clear if the two were had! The trip was over in a few days, and then it was back to the medical school and the usual grind.

The years went by. Some very famous personalities who taught in the university were seen, like Wynn Jones, who was a cardiologist, or Mr. Edwards, the cardiac surgeon. The latter was interesting in that he had a stethoscope, the end of which was almost touching the ground; that way he would not have to be too close to the patient when he was listening to their chest. He corrected a lot of Mitral Valves, one of the valves in the heart, as they quite often become narrow following streptococcal infection of the throat. He had to enter the heart with a fine knife closely attached to his finger and cut the narrowed segment.

As a part of one of the courses the students were to spend two months in Mill Road Hospital. The latter was women's hospital reserved for obstetrics. As part of the course each student had to do twenty normal and twenty abnormal deliveries during the period which was for about two months. That was not difficult, as there were about ten deliveries a day at the hospital! They also had the 'Flying Squad'; the latter is fully equipped with blood, oxygen and other resuscitation equipment and driven out wherever there were problems with home deliveries. Students had to accompany the obstetrician that went with the squad.

Instead of twenty deliveries of each kind, Govind did forty of each and wrote a paper that was impressive, and presented it to the teacher and the class at the end of the course. The course director did not show any signs that he was impressed by it, mainly as he appeared to have color prejudice.

There were generally groups of eight students that visited different hospitals, and in the process many in the group became good friends.

One member of the groups was John Beardsworth, who worked together with Govind for a long time. After qualifying, they did internships together. He also won a gold medal in pharmacology, and there were great hopes that he would eventually go into research after qualifying, but instead he went back to Blackpool, and became a General Practitioner. He got married and had children (he hated women! Could it be because he had many sisters?). His father was a Bank Manager in the town. He was a shy man, and when he was waiting for a bus at one time, Govind's wife was also waiting for the same bus, but he ignored her completely as though he did not know her and gave her a cold shoulder. However, it is not unlike the English to ignore anyone unless he or she has been properly introduced.

David Reitman was another very bigheaded person who became a psychiatrist eventually, was divorced twice, and is now settled in Newfoundland.

The number of interesting characters was numerous, but, because of their English upbringing which seems to encourage reticence, unfriendliness or whatever, it was not possible to continue friendship with but very few of the classmates.

CHAPTER 35

Hartington Road

L iving in the house in Botanic Gardens was not satisfactory, and Govind found accommodations in Hartington Road, a much nicer area of Liverpool. It was close to Sefton Park, which was a park with a large lake on which one could hire a boat at the marina and go rowing. It also had a statue of Eros (the other one being in London). It was also nice for a long walk.

Govind moved initially in the accommodations available at 139 Hartington Road. There were many students but the place was empty during the summer holidays. Govind, however continued his studies, and stayed there even during the holidays, mostly because he had nowhere else to go. A Mrs. Shoemaker, who was quite pleasant, owned the place and the food she made was good and tasty. Unfortunately, the prices she charged for accommodation were a bit high. She had a daughter, a Miss Evans, who was nice looking, and had a pleasant personality. She was always well dressed with a suit and jingled as she walked with all that jewelry she wore on her hands and body. She was also on a lookout for a husband. She had a daughter called Marlene, who was nine years old. Marlene was pretty and always well dressed. She loved to come and sit on Govind's lap, although she did not appreciate Govind's sweet odorous breath, which, as anyone knows, occurs after multiple snoozes! At one time she informed Govind that she would marry him if only she was not so young. How sweet, but children do say the nicest things.

❮❧o❦❯

Mrs. Williams (Willy)

O nce again Govind decided to move, as the meager amount of money coming from home was not sufficient to continue boarding at Mrs. Shoemaker's place. The money always came late, with the admonition that Govind should work and study, much like what many of the students did at the time, or so he assumed. It was impossible to convince Nanjibhai that that was not possible if one was to study Medicine.

At 141 Hartington Road, about three doors down, it was also possible to obtain accommodation. A Mrs. Williams ran the boarding house. She charged two pounds twelve shillings and sixpence a week. The charges were for a single room, with a heater in the room, as well as meals, i.e. breakfast, dinner and supper. Even in those days it was a fantastic deal.

Mrs. Williams, commonly referred to as 'Willy', was a personality. She was rather thin and wiry with a cigarette either in her hands or hanging from the side of her mouth, short, and bow legged. Well dressed with a blouse and skirt, but she wore slippers all the time. She smoked about sixty cigarettes a day. She also had a cat that was with her constantly. The cat had total freedom, including that of sniffing all the food, tasting it and generally approving it. She was a good cook and her food was probably made tastier by the fact that it was mixed with cigarette ashes, cat hair etc. She was generous with her servings.

There were numerous unforgettable characters that resided at this place. Charley resided there permanently, and it was thought that he was Willy's boyfriend, although no one dared to ask. There was Jim, who was a teacher who went to visit his girl friend in Wales every weekend, being about 100 miles away. It was said that she had Multiple Sclerosis, which came on a short time before they were to marry. They never married but he stayed ever faithful to her. It was very touching. There was Ian who was a football coach. There was a teacher called Mr. Stainsbury. No one knew his first name. He rode around on a powerful motorcycle. There was an unforgettable girl called Mary. She had swollen eyes, and it appeared that she was reading too much, day and late at night, and without doing any other exercise or any other activities. It appeared that she knew everything, and she knew that she knew it, and showed it. Often she would straighten out what anyone said, and loved contradicting everyone. As one can imagine, the room was all silent when she appeared, or even became empty in a short while after her appearance.

Maganlal, Govind's younger brother finished his schooling in Nairobi, and came to Liverpool, and was admitted in the University of Liverpool, faculty of Laws to study for the degree of LLB, and become a Lawyer. He joined the residence at Hartington Road and began his studies. He took rides on Govind's motorcycle quite often. At one time the two decided to take a ride to Birmingham and see Lalji. The motorcycle was going well, except when a hill came along. The engine got too hot and just stopped. Govind was able to start it, but it did not have much power, so Maganlal had to run along and push it as Govind was driving it—it was strenuous for Maganlal, if not comical.

CHAPTER 37

❧❀☙

Affairs of the Heart

There is no man or woman who has not undergone a heat that is hotter than the hottest erupting volcano, or a coolness that is cooler than the coolest environment encountered on the zenith of Mt. Everest, metaphorically speaking. Love is thought to be residing in the heart as one feels the flutter, the occasional stoppage, or the racing of the heart, but it is in fact the brain that feels the elation or depression as a direct result of the beauty seen in the opposite sex. No doubt the raging hormones that are in the body as well other factors, such as age, religion, caste, color, environment etc. also play a part, and modify it.

Govind was intent on his Medical Studies, and felt that nothing else should come in the way of his prime objective. He also felt that it would be less of a problem for the future if he married an Indian girl. There were some beautiful girls in England who were prepared to go out on a date with him, but his shyness, and the other factors mentioned, prevented it. During some of his vacations, he took trips to Kenya, and of course many fathers of a daughter felt that there was not a better catch than that of a doctor or one training to be a doctor. He was visiting Mombasa once, and a pretty girl called Manjula had come to see him and introduce herself. Though her looks were out of this world, and her lovely fragrance all pervading, Govind was too shy even to converse with her, so he just put his shoes on and left. The memory was that of her footwear lying at the entrance of the house.

At another time, he was visiting a family in Mombasa, a town that is on the shore of the Indian Ocean. He was introduced to a girl called Dinbala. She was a girl of enormous beauty, or so he thought, superb intelligence, with bright intelligent eyes and mannerisms that conquered the mind and heart of anyone who met her. Her father was called Damji Lila Gohil. There were four brothers, the eldest was Natha Lila, the next one was the Damjibhai, mentioned above; the third one was Govind Lila and the last one was Jadavji Lila. The two eldest hated the other two, although the reason for the hate was not clear, but so much so that they would not participate in any functions even a marriage if it was in the family of the opposite side. The eldest, Mr. Natha Lila had a heart attack, and was stuck to his bed for fourteen years. He was always afraid that one day he would die in bed when no one was present. As fate would have it, that was exactly what happened! He died in bed, all-alone, while the family had gone to a wedding.

The Gohil family business was that of heavy canvas and other heavy materials like sails and such like needed for ships etc. Damjibhai, as per custom, every day after closing the shop, took all the accounts and other books for his older brother's perusal at his residence. He worked very hard, and was often lumbered with backaches. He had many treatments, including primitive systems like producing scars on the back by means of a hot poker, and the reduction of a 'pechoty', the latter being some form of treatment that can only be given by a person who himself or herself was a breech delivery. Sometimes they tie the big toe of the right leg with string after the treatment, so that the 'pechoty', which is in the abdomen, does not slip! At times it is tied so tight that the toe can become black or gangrenous, and painful because of poor circulation! He also took a liking to whiskey, which not only dulled his pains, but also improved his tortured mind. He would at times come home inebriated, and was a little hard on his wife or his eldest son, although he never was the same on his daughters. He was rather strong, and the abuse sustained by the sufferers could be extensive. One day he was having some heart pains, so at lunchtime, he went and saw his family doctor, who advised him to go home and rest. He did, but he rested forever. After going to bed, he turned to one side, snored a few times rather heavily, frothed at the mouth and said goodbye to the world. It was rather sad, as he was well liked by the town's people, who called him 'kaka'—or uncle. The third brother, Govind Kara had the bad habit of gambling, losing money, and drinking at the same time. One night he was totally inebriated, and his wife had placed their baby close to him. It was a big mistake, as when he turned, his heavy leg went on the child's mouth and stayed there for the night. The child was found dead in the morning.

It was interesting that although the men of the households carried on their feuds, but the women and children were comfortable socializing with each other.

❧০❧

CHAPTER 38

Hitched

Govind was in Liverpool when the offer in the form of a letter arrived. He was informed that Mr. Damji Lila was interested in his daughter Dinbala becoming engaged to Govind, if he was interested. A photograph of this angel had accompanied the letter. Interested, interested—what mundane words! The sky opened up and a bright rainbow appeared and the heart began to sing. He had to slow down, collect his wits and of course agree to the offer that was the most momentous decision of his life. The engagement ceremonies were held in Kenya in his absence. Of course, then correspondence was in order—he wrote letters, poems, and sonnets, with good replies. To telephone in those days was impossible, as the charges were exorbitant. Life changed for Govind from then on.

The name Dinbala was shortened at times to Dinu, or Din, as time flew by.

CHAPTER 39

❖

Govind becomes a Doctor

It was a momentous month—the month of July 1958. Govind gave his examinations in Medicine, Surgery, Obstetrics and Gynecology. He qualified as a doctor, and obtained his degrees in Bachelor of Medicine and Bachelor of Surgery—M.B., Ch.B. for short.

A year's internship is required before one can work with the public as a full-fledged doctor. He knew that because of being colored, the chances of working in prestigious hospitals like the Royal Infirmary were out of the question. He, along with his friend, John Beardsworth, applied at Whiston Hospital, which is a part of the Lancashire Group of Hospital. The Hospital was situated in Prescot, Lancashire. A Dr. Chisholm interviewed them. It was a successful interview, and the two were informed that they could start their jobs in September.

There was a break for two months before starting. Govind's father sent him a ticket to visit the family, and also get married. The arrangements began as soon as he got to Kenya. Govind's mother was beaming with pride. She was a gentle character, full of sayings, and never had a bad word to say about anyone. The wedding party started off in about a dozen cars on the dusty road to Mombasa. The road itself is a nightmare to travel on. Jamnadas thought he would take the short cut, and took a different route. On the road, he drove the car into a lake. It was quite a job to pull it out. On reaching Mombasa, he had no interest in attending the wedding, so he took a group of his friends and went to the seashore and had a party of his own making. Govind was dressed in a white 'China' suit, and a 'Nehru' cap. The only problem was that the food in Mombasa always upset him, and he was liable to have an upset stomach, and bouts of diarrhea. Fortunately, the wedding ceremony was a short one, and lasted only an hour in the afternoon. The ceremony was also conducted while the couple sat on a sofa, which was rare in those days. It was a very impressive Hindu ceremony. The couple had a chance to meet with all the family members and her friends. Photographs were taken. Once again the journey to Nyeri was undertaken, with an extra broken hearted and torn person being on board. However, there was a surprise party at the border of the town, when the opposing party brought food and drinks for the party that was leaving.

The party reached home the next day at 4 a.m., and of course there is another game to be played by the new husband and wife. Gold rings are put in opaque colored water in a large dish and after throwing the dice to see who goes first, then the person elected moves his or her hand around the dish and fishes out the jewelry. The one who fishes it out gets to keep it; not only that, but, it is said that that person will rule the roost in the future. It wasn't Govind who won the throw.

After a few days the heavenly honeymoon was over, and the couple flew back to Britain. Once again a visit was made to the venerable Colonial Office, who gave the firm admonition that the two should not even have come to England. There was no hope for Dinu to join any hospital to follow a course in nursing. She cried buckets of tears on leaving the office, and was inconsolable despite being told that many hospitals were short of nurses, and the first hospital that was approached would take her in. They stayed at the house of a nice lady called Mrs. Hasuben Parikh, and after a few days left for the city of Liverpool. In Liverpool, they approached the Matron of Broadgreen Hospital, who was glad to admit Dinu into the Nursing program. Only problem was that she was not eighteen yet, so she would have to serve as a Cadet Nurse. She accepted it and started the course soon afterwards. However, it turned out to be a chore, as it consisted of cleaning bottles, and taking messages to different departments. She felt that her time was being wasted as at home she was in teacher's training, and was doing well. However, stoically, as per her strong character, she overtook this minor problem, and started the Nursing Program in earnest.

Govind had sold his motorcycle by then.

CHAPTER 40

❮❦०❧❯

Whiston Hospital, Prescot, Lancashire

As one drives from Liverpool, after passing the town of Prescot, one is on the road leading to St. Helens, and after passing the town, one turned right to go to the hospital, while turning left took one to the nurses' residence. On turning right one went into the main road of the hospital, and on taking this road, on the left side were numerous wards, mostly ugly flat prefabricated buildings, while on the right was the dining room, and further down were the labs and the Auxiliary Hospital.

Working at the hospital consisted in rotating internships of six months of medicine and six months of surgery. In addition there was an on call rota, which consisted of being on duty every other day. It also included working in the Emergency Department. There were no pagers in those days, so there were various color lights at every corner. You were assigned certain combination of lights.

There were numerous doctors working at the hospital—junior and senior house officers, junior and senior registrars, junior and senior consultants, as well as fully equipped pathology laboratories with its own personnel, laundry, housing for other important departments etc.

Work at the hospital started in earnest. It was also a harrowing experience. It also turned out to be quite an experience. The numbers of diseases that presented in the Emergency Dept. were enormous and challenging. There was a colliery nearby, called Cronton Colliery, which produced coal. Some of the workers who came as patients presented with heart rending problems like chronic cough, wheezing, shortness of breath, bronchitis, emphysema and many other chest problems. There were also many other problems. Some were even brought in dead, the result of a collapsed roof while working in a confined space. Injuries of all kinds presented themselves.

At one time some gangsters were fighting, and one person who was brought into emergency had fallen backwards onto a window and broke the glass, an end of which penetrated his chest. The brilliant senior registrar immediately diagnosed it as pneumothorax and drained his chest, revealing a large amount of blood in his chest cavity. He was otherwise going into cardiac failure and would have died. Many an asthmatic presented a heavy and wheezing chest that needed immediate intravenous therapy in the form of bronchodilators, antibiotics etc. One time in the middle of the night there was a call from Sister Eardley, the pleasant lady who had earned the Victoria Cross during the war. She was in charge of a ward. She informed Govind that she had a patient in the Auxiliary that was vomiting blood. Govind saw the patient immediately and formed an opinion that the vomitus was not blood, so he took a specimen of the material to the lab, and checked it under a microscope and noted that it was nothing but a reddish pudding he had ingested the night before. This was done at about three in the morning. It was an achievement that scored high marks for him. His consultant, a Dr. Thelwall Jones was very impressed and made it a point of mentioning it during his next day's 'ward round'. There was another patient who was on the second floor who had threatened that he would commit suicide by throwing himself through a window, so he was moved to the main floor. He underwent some testing and was declared to be quite safe, so he was sent back to the second floor, and sure enough, on the second day he opened a window and jumped out. He hit the road below and said goodbye to the world. At one time Govind had to go and see a patient who could not pass water. And indeed, the bladder was overfull. He asked for a long needle, and plunged it through the abdomen into the bladder. A large amount of urine poured out and the patient breathed a sigh of relief. Govind was feeling good until the next day when his registrar told him that he might have caused a fistula, a permanent opening from the bladder to the outside world.

Mehdiratta was a surgeon in training, and had come from India. Very conscientious, but had no clue at times how to proceed. Sometimes what would happen in the middle of an operation, after he had made his incision, opened the abdomen and had all the guts out, he would have no idea how to proceed. Then he would have to call his consultant who would advise him how to proceed, over the phone! He eventually obtained his FRCS. In England one is not called a 'Doctor' but a 'Mister' after passing his fellowship examination. He was upset as many still called him 'Doctor', even though he had conquered the mountain. He had a girlfriend who was a nurse. She lived in the Nurses Residence. He would often call Govind and ask if he would drive him and his girlfriend in his car, across to the Nurses residence so the security people at the entrance to the residence would not notice the girl hiding in the back seat. He was once invited for dinner in Govind's apartment by his family, where, after dinner, he wanted everyone to leave so that he would have the apartment to himself and his girl friend so they could have some fun!

Food at the hospital was excellent. The 'fridge' was always kept full of food in case any doctor wanted to cook by himself. It was open all the time so that whoever was hungry could go to the kitchen and help himself or even cook a meal for his liking. Dinu was an expert cook as part of her training in Mombasa. She had taken home sciences, which included cooking. Many times she took great pleasure in the kitchen and of course pleased many stomachs.

She used to come by bus from Broadgreen Hospital, beautifully dressed with a colorful sari, often green and made of silk, or red pants and a black sweater. There was a conductor who noticed her getting off at the bus stop at the hospital, and asked her at one time if her dad was getting better after all that devotion!

Govind rented a small apartment at Huyton (the place where Mr. Wilson, the Prime Minister of Britain had come from). Huyton was some distance from Liverpool and about eight miles from Prescot. He had a bicycle then, and he used to cycle from the apartment to the hospital, wheezing and struggling away because of his asthma and what with all the smog and a heavily polluted environment. Maganlal had joined the two and lived in the apartment at the time.

CHAPTER 41

❦

A Car

There was a Dr. Rosenthal at the Hospital who was the proud possessor of a Hillman Humber, 1940 Model. Its engine purred like a cat, and the color was dull green. He was selling it for 100 British Pounds. Govind wrote home for some money, for at a salary of 35 Pounds a month, there was no saving, especially not anything left over for buying a car. His father once again came to the rescue, and sent him some money to buy the car. He bought the car. At the time, if one went to the offices of the Automobile Association and informed them that he was from overseas and used to have a license abroad, which was tongue in cheek and of course was a lie, he would get a license to drive for a year. It is how he obtained a driver's license for a year. On the first day he drove the car, he drove it to show off his new acquisition to his brother who lived on Hartington Road at the time. On leaving the hospital, the cop gave a signal for Govind to proceed, but he did not know that Govind had no idea about gears, accelerator, etc., to go ahead, but somehow he managed, with a great deal of trepidation.

The car was rather interesting, and it would appear that no other car in the world was like it. The floor was rusty, and in some parts of the bodywork was totally corroded, with large irregular holes on the floor making it drafty and cold, especially the feet of anyone who dared to sit in the car. A paraffin heater was placed on the floor on the passenger side for Dinu. The windscreen wiper worked manually by the passenger, utilizing the circular knob that was in the center on the dashboard. Often the car refused to start and one had to go out and turn the crankcase by means of the handle that dangled in the front. The engine worked fine after it was started. When he drove down to Broadgreen Hospital to visit his wife, and if he saw any nurses at the bus stop, (and there were always quite a few), he would give them all a ride. They were packed in like sardines. There was also on average a puncture every five miles, making Govind an expert at changing tires. At one time he just went ahead with black paint and brush and painted the car black. It was not a bad job. There were small garages at one end meant for parking cars overnight. Once on entering the garage, the back of the car was angled instead of straight, and it hit the upright beam of the shed, and the back mudguard came off, not surprising because of all that rust. No problem, Govind went to the X-Ray Department and borrowed some old X-Rays, taped them nicely so that it would look like a mudguard and painted it black. It looked good and Govind was proud of his achievement. He thought it looked like a masterpiece.

At one time Dinbala expressed a desire to learn to drive. Govind rather proudly explained to her all about gears, steering, and other workings of the car. She was rather exasperated and said she did not want to know all that, and that she only wanted to drive. So she was allowed to do so, and she drove the car straight on to a mound of gravel where the car engine sputtered and died.

There was a heavy fog one evening, and Govind had dropped Dinbala at her hospital that night. On entering the divided highway, the visibility was very poor, and he, without realizing, started to drive on the wrong side of the highway. Realizing it, he immediately turned the car and went over a large mound dividing the highway, coming down with a crash on the other side. It was a hairy situation.

One day the two decided to drive to London. Dinbala kept her legs warm with the heater, as she worked the knob to clear the windscreen of all that rain that was pouring outside. Eventually they reached Hasuben Parikh's house, and, after an overnight stay, the two started off again to return to Liverpool. After saying their goodbyes, the two took off, and reached St. Albans where they came across a T-Junction where, instead of turning right, they turned left. On the road, they had a puncture, and Govind changed the tire in pouring rain; then they continued driving, and where do they end up but Goldersgreen—Hasuben's place! It was disappointing to end up where they started initially but once again they took off. They did not take the wrong turn this time when they came to St. Albans!

Early one morning in Huyton where the family lived, Govind saw a policeman looking at his car rather intensely. The car was parked properly so Govind approached him confidently.

"Excuse me sir, is this your car?' asked the policeman. The answer was in the affirmative.

"Well sir, there are many defects in it that make it dangerous on the road. Perhaps I can point these out to you."

He went around the car, and pointed out the many jagged pieces of metal sticking out. He showed the tires that were thin and bulging in certain areas. He asked Govind to go inside and pull the handbrake, and he pushed the car at the same time. The car moved without effort.

He pulled out a notebook, and wrote down all the defects. He then issued a summons to Govind. He was summoned at a court hearing in Prscot to which he did not go, as he had pleaded guilty to all counts. He was fined six pounds on each count. He also got the defects repaired, but after a while, he could not stand the car any longer, so he took it to the scrap yard. He was paid five pounds for that. The check appeared in the mail some months later. It was reported in the local newspaper called the Huyton Chronicle that a medical student was fined such and such amount for possessing a dangerous car. They did not dare to mention that it was a doctor at the local Hospital.

CHAPTER 42

A Tragedy at Whiston Hospital

The tragedy happened at Whiston Hospital. The Hospital Administrator, a Mr. Lawson, was a man of considerable repute and outstanding in the community. He had a daughter called Barbara—a very nice and pretty young woman. She fell in love with the registrar in the ear and nose department. His name was Mr. Mohamed El Rifi. She had become pregnant, and it presented her boyfriend with a dilemma. Knowledge of her being pregnant would raise her father's ire, and it was possible that the good doctor would be deported to his country of origin. The couple was not married and did not wish to bring up a child. Dr. El Rifi took her to his room, and talked her into having an abortion, a procedure he carried out by some primitive means. Things went horribly wrong and she started to bleed profusely vaginally. From the doctor's room, she was immediately transferred to the I.C.U., which was just across the road. Despite heroic efforts, the girl did not survive, and was pronounced dead soon afterwards. Mo (as he was called) was taken by the police, and locked up in detention. David who was his friend, went to see if he could help his friend. He saw the police and informed him that he would look after his friend at his home until the case came up. The police agreed to the suggestion, and handed over the gentleman to his care. While in David's house, he went to use the bathroom. He saw a shaving blade on the sink. With the blade he slashed his wrist, and bled to death. After all the time it took to break the lock in the bathroom to be able to open the door, he was found dead. He was lying on the floor crumpled up with a large pool of blood beside him, the result of a slashed wrist that was obviously self-inflicted. It was a tragedy that should never have happened.

The tragic death of two innocent and promising lives should make us all pause for a moment and see if our laws can be changed in order that this form of tragedy does not happen again.

CHAPTER 43

❖

Whiston Hospital, Prescot, Lancashire (continued)

Internship at the Hospital, as mentioned earlier, was to follow the vocation of medicine for six months and then surgery for six months. It was hard work, but the reward was a wealth of practical experience. Seeing patients at night gave some patients the impression that the doctor was trying to make an extra 'package' for working so late, but in fact that was not true. An unbelievable variety of diseases affecting people were seen in medicine. There were Syphilitics (thank God the disease of Syphilis is almost wiped out from the earth mainly due to of penicillin), poliomyelitis—both acute and chronic types, with some patients on the 'Iron Lung Machines' (the contraption that helped the patients to breathe), and these patients had to use them all their life! Tuberculosis of all types with severely scarred lungs, patients with cancers of all kinds etc. were also seen and treated, under supervision of course. The doctors that were on duty had to attend to all the cases that presented at the hospital. Surgery was even more taxing. The consultant in charge, a Mr. Richard Doyle (or Dicky Doyle as many called him) was a workaholic. His surgical lists, which ran twice a week, started in the afternoon at 2 p.m. and ran well into the night till about ten p.m. This happened twice a week with regularity. Apart from the 'lists', there were emergency surgeries to be performed every day, after a full consultation and investigations, all done late at night. It seems that he did not reach home to enjoy any form of a family life. He fell in love with the 'sister' that was in the operating room, who was with him all the time, even when not working. Sometimes he used to take her out for dinner after his list. He divorced his wife and eventually married his love.

One evening, Govind received a telephone call from the British Army to tell him that he was to join the National Service for two years after completing his job at the Hospital. The service was mandatory. Govind informed them that he had enrolled in the School of Tropical Medicine in Liverpool, and after completion of the course he would contact them. The said school was world renowned, and he had in fact applied at the school to undergo the course that was offered, which was in tropical medicine and hygiene. A letter confirming that he was accepted had come sometime later.

After competing his job at Whiston Hospital, he was given the certificate that attested that he was now a full-fledged doctor and enabled him to practice Medicine, Surgery, Obstetrics and Gynecology and related pursuits. The family continued living in Huyton, and Dinbala continued her work at Broadgreen Hospital. Govind started to follow his course in tropical medicine and hygiene. It was a very intensive course, and the variety of diseases to be seen and learn about was enormous. As an example, they showed the famous tsetse fly, the one that causes trypanosomiasis, or sleeping sickness, whereby the affected patient has an infection of his brain and eventually succumbs to the disease. The trypanosome is a parasite that lives in the fly, and is introduced to the host. The fly has a typical hatchet shaped veins on its wings. It affects cattle also, and because of it, vast stretches of Africa are barren. Also to be seen were Hookworms, Roundworms, Filaria, and Tapeworms from beef and pork termed Tenia Solium and Tenia Saginatta respectively; Onchocerciasis—the ones whose progeny causes river blindness, Bilharzia, the scourge of Africa. The disease as evidenced by the fact that they were passing blood in the urine affected at one time 80 % of Egyptians. They were shown the fly called Simulium Damnosum, the one that causes Dengue, and different types of mosquito that cause malaria, yellow fever etc.

One of the teachers was Professor Maigraith, who had come from Australia. A tall man that looked burly, but in fact very friendly. He wore a Harris Tweed jacket with patches at the elbow. It was part of his clothing every day. He had a large nodule over the left eyebrow. Under the skin of the nodule, it was said that there was the worm of onchocerca volvulus, the progeny of which cause river blindness. He had injected himself with the worm so he can study it better. Whenever the worm caused problems to his health, he used to get treatment, but just enough to paralyze the worm, and then he would study it further. This was rather like the story of John Hunt (a famous surgeon in London) who had given himself syphilis on his penis to study the disease. He then used to treat himself with mercury or arsenic as need be, just enough to make himself better, but not eradicate the disease. These worms are minute and are often seen in the eye as it travels in the anterior chamber or the conjunctiva where it can be seen and removed by means of surgery. He is also the main character involved with regards to the Irish Giant.

The story of Burke and Hare comes to mind. The couple ran a rooming house in Edinburgh, Scotland. At that time the university was in short supply of human cadavers, and paid handsomely for them. The couple obliged by supplying the corpses. They would take in for room and board vagrants that were in the city. At night they would murder them by dragging them across the floor, and after making sure that they were dead, sell them to the medical school in the morning. It gave them quite a comfortable living.

The story of Rodney crops up once again at this junction.

Rodney had also booked for the course, but he came two weeks late as he had been on his honeymoon. The course was only for four months. He was very bright as evidenced by the fact that he took away the gold medal in Tropical Medicine, and the silver medal in Tropical Hygiene at the completion of the course! It was unbelievable. He became the professor of genetics in the University of Manchester but has retired now. He lost his first wife to cancer, and now he is married to Hilary, who is a medical practitioner in Manchester, and a beautiful person. Unfortunately, during medical student days, he was deaf in his right ear, and over the years, he has also become deaf in his left ear. However, he manages well, and has a 'hearing dog' now. The dog tells him whenever the front doorbell rings, or the telephone rings, or if there is any sound that needs attention. The couple has no children.

A word in praise of dogs—there is no better companion that man can have that is better than a dog.

At completion of the course and appropriate examinations, Govind obtained the Diploma in Tropical Medicine and Hygiene (D.T.M. &H.).

He had no desire to join the British Army, and started making preparations to leave the country. Dinbala was about two years away to being an S.R.N. (State Registered Nurse) at the time. Unfortunately she had to resign from her course.

Booking was made to travel to Kenya by ship, the one that was called Kenya Castle. The ship belonged to the Cunard Lines of Liverpool.

RETURN TO KENYA

CHAPTER 44

❮✄o✁❯

Return to Kenya

H.M.S. Kenya Castle

Dinbala resigned her post and the couple made preparations to travel to Kenya and leave Liverpool. She was pregnant at the time. The couple's first child, a daughter that they named Sheila (meaning, 'the one who gives beauty') was born in Mombasa. The first port of call was Genoa, where the ship anchored for three days. The local markets were interesting. Being bored, the couple went to see a movie, a film that was called Twenty Thousand Leagues Under the Sea. After booking, they had to go through a corridor for about two hundred yards before reaching the actual theatre. Unfortunately the movie was in Italian, and therefore a little hard to follow but it was not hard to get the gist of the story. It did not subtitles

The ship ploughed through the Mediterranean Sea to the Port of Alexandria. A bus trip was taken to Cairo, to see the world famous Sphinx and the Pyramids at Giza. The approach was by means of a camel ride from a suburb of Cairo, and the owners of these camels take the gullible tourists to one side and ask for a 'baksheesh' (a little bribery). The one who did not give the baksheesh was in bad books indeed! The guide as well as the camel became bad tempered if no baksheesh was given!

One of the passengers that became very friendly was a Mr. Bali, who was an Inspector of Police on the Island of Zanzibar. He teased the couple quite often but it was obvious that he was taken in by Dinbala's beauty. The Port of Mombasa was reached eventually, and the couple took the train journey to Nairobi, where Jamnadas, his older brother, picked them up.

Govind at one time went to Zanzibar along with Jamnadas who was exhausted from work and needed a holiday badly. They booked in a hotel, but contacted Mr. Bali while they were there. He was gracious enough to invite the two brothers for dinner. Mr. Bali was the inspector of police for the town of Zanzibar. It was interesting, as there is a petrol shortage on the Island, so every time he went downhill, he would shut off the engine and let the car coast along.

His wife had cooked up a good chicken curry, but she did not sit along with the others at the table, as per Muslim custom. As soon as the duo left, there were riots in the town between the local natives and Arabs, and 80% of the world's supply of cloves—a form of spice that is used in cooling—was destroyed.

Dinbala went to Mombasa as it is the custom for Hindus that for delivery of the first child the wife has to go to her parent's house. The little girl was born in Mombasa, and was called Sheila. She was born in the Pandya Clinic. The clinic is well known in the town. It is run by Maharashtrians, a man and wife team called Dr. Curve and his wife who was known as Kashiben. Kashiben in fact did all the work associated with the delivery of a baby. He was also a family practitioner, and did a number of house calls every day. His son Madhav Curve had become a cardiologist and joined the clinic. (At one time, a large number of Morphine syringes that were used up were found in the toilet. It was suspected that one of the Doctors at the clinic had been using it.) In those years Kenya was becoming very unstable, and after the death of his parents, he had decided to emigrate to Texas in America. However, he never made it, as he, along with his whole family were murdered the day before they were to travel. All the family was hacked to death. Sometimes the cruelties of mankind are unfathomable, as illustrated here. The family was murdered with multiple cuts with a 'panga', which is somewhat like a machete, but is curved and sharpened on one side only. It was done in cold blood and with no real rewards to be had.

Jamnadas picked up the couple and they went to Nyeri via Saba Saba, Fort Hall, Maragua, and Karatina. On the way to Nyeri, Govind could feel an undercurrent of unhappiness in the family, and a dislike by different members of the family for each other.

CHAPTER 45

❮ ❧o❧ ❯

General Practice in Kenya

On reaching Nyeri, Govind had made up his mind that he should locate in that particular town and start General Practice there. Mr. Nanjibhai owned the building where the Ladies Tailoring House was located. Next to the store but in the same property was a small shop for a barber, the next one was empty, and after that one was a grocery store owned by a Mr. Desai. The shop was called Lenana Grocers. Next to the building was the big post office of Nyeri. Govind decided to take up the empty space. The office was rent-free. The carpenters moved in, and worked day and night and constructed exactly as Govind wanted it to be. Beyond the front partition, which was about twelve feet from the entrance, was a small opening that could be closed if need be and in that area was a small pharmacy; then there were three rooms for consultations and treatments, and then the office at the back. The rooms had surgical instruments, a microscope, and a leather bed for examination and treatment. In one corner was built a small area for sterilization of syringes and some storage. There was a mall stove on which was a pan of water, in which the metal syringes were boiled and sterilized. At the main entrance was a big picture of Govind taken in Liverpool at his graduation. Dinbala's sister, Chandri had made two beautiful pictures, one of a child that was dirty, filthy, swarming with flies, while the other one was that of a smart boy going to school, and the caption was 'kana gaku ne kariku', in other words 'which one is your child?' The carpenters who were very efficient and quick were 'Cutchis'—they come from Cutch in India.

General Practice started in earnest. The patients were mostly African, but there were some Asians and Europeans also. The Africans were very poor, but straightforward, and paid up without any hassles, if they had the money. Some said that they could not afford the treatment when it was given for free.

The practice was busy from the beginning. Govind searched for malarial parasites in the blood of many a patient, only to learn some months later that the area was malaria free! Many of the diseases were those of poverty—coughs and colds, pneumonia, malnutrition with Kwashiorkor, diarrhea and vomiting, whooping cough, measles, round worms, toxoplasmosis, syphilis, gonorrhea, etc.

Two nurses were hired—Mrs. Festus, and Mrs. Dudson. Mr. Wachera commonly referred to as 'Papdo' ('Papad' in Indian means a big chip!) was hired to look after the cleanliness of the office and looking after the patient's comfort. He formed a habit of going to the market and telling many that there was a new doctor in town that could cure them of their maladies with just one injection.

The Kikuyu tribe, the main inhabitants of the Central Province of Kenya is a race like no other. They have a dowry system, but it is reversed, in that the man pays for a wife to the woman's parents in the way of so many sheep, goats, cattle etc. He is allowed more than one wife, and is considered rich if he has many wives, as they do all the work, including farming, etc. They believe in male circumcision, and, unfortunately some still carry out female circumcision, a horrendous practice that at times leads to the loss of a life. The slavery many women undergo is unbelievable. Sometimes they go collecting wood and take it home with them. The wood is carried with leather straps that go around the wood, extending from one end to another, and then the weight of the bundle is carried on the head. Years of this form of slavery leave deep dents on the wearer's skull, as well as a bent posture, and loss of all hair from the scalp. Many of them develop a permanent kyphosis, whereby the whole body stays bent forwards.

Their language is beautiful, rather lilting, with many sayings thrown in. Acting out of words often follows their speech. As an example:

'Aterere, ne re', in other words—'I am telling you, listen to me', 'ne karwadu muno'—'I am very sick'. Continuing the explanation may be:

'Ne Nyoka, ne wasie haha, ne sie haha', 'Ne homa muno', which means, 'There is a big snake in my body, and it slithers and moves around and ends up here' as he points out different areas of his body. 'Ne homa muno', in other words, then I have a bad fever, and burn up my whole being'.

Mrs. Dudson translates all that. Not only that, but she acts it out, and what a show she puts on with all the contortions she gives to her own body. It was rather like a dance and very interesting, and Govind watched her with some fascination. The lady is a sweet little thing. It is amazing how little the paychecks of all the workers are, and even then they seem to manage despite the fact that they have such a small budget to work with. Mrs. Dudson is always smartly dressed, caring and nurturing her family, punctual at work, etc.

Amazingly, she, along with many others has a permanent smile on them without even a glint of their difficulties being apparent.

A diagnosis is made, and the patient is informed about the cost of the treatment. It often involves an injection, generally of penicillin, and/or chloroquine, sulphonamide tablets (generally a sulpha drug made by May & Baker, called 693 (very popular in those days, and all Africans knew about it, and even asked for it by name!)), and tablets of APC, i.e. Aspirin, Phenacetin, and Codeine. It was a wonderful combination, and cured many illnesses. The charge for all the treatment was 10 Shillings, about a quarter of a Canadian dollar. Even in those days it was cheap, and there was no real profit involved.

There were venereal diseases, and the patients with this disorder insisted on seeing the doctor by themselves and privately. Generally they came at the end of the month after receiving their salaries, and of course the quoted treatment with penicillin and other drugs went up tenfold. (Maybe reminiscent of Robin Hood?) The treatment of gonorrhea, which was very common, with pus pouring out from the genitals, was with antibiotics, but they all felt better if some gentian violet was applied to the affected areas.

The test for syphilis was the Kahn test, expressed as +, or ++ or +++ depending on the severity of the disease. It was not uncommon to have three pluses with many patients.

The Provincial Hospital in Nyeri was very busy with many doctors that were employed there. However, the number of patients seeking treatment was overwhelming at the hospital and also at the doctor's offices.

There were many young boys who would come rather sheepishly and ask if the good doctor performed circumcision. The answer being in the affirmative, the procedure was carried out for 25 shillings. (The Provincial Hospital carried it out for thirty shillings). Govind obtained fishing nylon from his father's shop, and sterilized it by means of the boiling water, and used it for suture. An anesthetic injection at the base of the penis with Procaine Amide gave excellent anesthesia. As the penis is quite vascular, one has to make sure that there no bleeders that were left untied. There was a patient he saw some years later—the nylon had migrated into his Penis, and could be felt under the skin, but was not really bothering him. Of course no woman can be present in the surgery, so the great papdo was enlisted for the job. Unfortunately he thought he was carrying out the surgery, which made it rather amusing at times!

Papdo used to wash the clinic floor daily. He would sweep the floor of all the red dirt first, and then wash it with soap and water. He was told not to sweep it dry as it created a lot of dust but he would not listen. The Doctor had developed chronic sinusitis and asthma because of all that allergenic dust and dirt that was in the air. So before Papdo started to clean the place, he would just leave the office. In later years, he would go home and collect his daughter Sheila and they would go for a ride in the country, towards Mathari Mission and Tetu Hills.

A record was made of each patient that presented consisting of their name, address, diagnosis and investigations undertaken, the treatment given and the amounts charged etc.

(Coins in Kenya were interesting, in that all of them had a hole punched out in the center, the idea being that all of them could be put together with a string, which is then put around the neck, rather like a necklace!).

CHAPTER 46

Sick Children

There is nothing more disheartening than to see a child suffering, especially when it is from a sickness that is preventable. There were many children who were presented by the parents in the office because of severe whooping cough, or diarrhea and vomiting, malnutrition etc. Because of these illnesses, Govind started a free clinic to immunize children against the dreaded diseases like diphtheria, whooping cough, and tetanus, with so-called 'triple' vaccine. Unfortunately, the supply was limited so each child received a quarter of the dose required.

One day a man brought his baby with the story that the child had roundworms. The child was given a dose of Piperazine to drink in the office, as he could not afford the full dose that should be used at home. He returned the next day, bursting with pride and happiness, as the child had passed 35 roundworms in his stools the next day. He actually got down and counted them!

There was a child brought in with a history of fevers, difficulty breathing etc. It was obvious that the child had bronchitis with early pneumonia. Appropriate medicines were given, but the child was presented on the next day and was obviously worse. Govind offered to take the child to the hospital along with the dad. The child was admitted, and the father was offered a lift back to the town. On the way back, he argued that he had spent the money unnecessarily with Govind, as the child was if anything, worse. He was happy when his five shillings were returned.

CHAPTER 47

Sterile Women

Many women had presented in the office because of the fact that they were unable to conceive. A simple treatment was given for these women. An apparatus was put together which consisted of a canula attached to a long tube, and the canula was inserted into the cervical canal of the uterus. Air was insufflated through it with an insuflator, while listening to the abdomen. Air is heard gurgling in, and tends to open out the passages. It is remarkable how many women became pregnant following the procedure.

One female patient had come to the office. She was about six months pregnant and had come for a checkup. 'This is the woman that you got pregnant', said the nurse. She was technically correct but amusing.

CHAPTER 48

❧❦०❦❧

Ophthalmology

As time passed, and as he was seeing more and more cases with eye problems, he started to develop interest in eye diseases. He drove down to Nanyuki to see an ophthalmologist called Dr. Singh and see him perform cataract surgery. This in itself was quite an achievement, as he had tried to see a Dr. T0lya, an eye surgeon of considerable repute in Nairobi, and in particular see him perform eye surgery, without any success. It is amazing how protective many doctors and others are in their little empires and do not wish it for anyone to learn their techniques or methods of approach to different diseases.

Dr Singh was quite a gentleman. Unfortunately, his problem was alcohol, combined with the fact that he used drive to Nairobi every weekend. Once his car overturned as he was driving, and that was the end of Dr. Singh.

Govind decided to order all the necessary instruments for cataract surgery such as the Von Graefe knife, the Iris Forceps, and a box of Lenses etc. He developed a dark room where he carried out retinoscopy, which consists of having a powerful light above and behind patient's left shoulder, and by means of a circular mirror, which has a hole in it, and shining it on a patient's eye, and movements of the light reflex giving an indication of the type of glasses a patient may need. He developed eye charts, and placed them twenty feet from the patient to be examined. By putting appropriate lenses in front of the patient, one could assess the strength of the glasses a patient would need. All the knowledge was derived from an old book, called Neame and Noble, published in 1939! The practice was in the early 60s! Even for that time the book was primitive.

Nanjibhai one day collected an old lady who lived in a hut by herself. She was totally blind with mature Cataracts. Her life was very hard, as she was poor, and many children went near her hut and teased her incessantly. She was brought in for Cataract surgery. Even before starting the procedure, she said she wanted to go to the toilet, but in fact she was scared. Then the anesthetic injection was given, but by that time even the Doctor was scared and the procedure was abandoned, with the relief of all!

There was a Somali who was also blind, and was led around town by children. He had a stick in his hand and a child who led him grabbed the other end of the stick. He came often to enquire as to when he can have his cataract removed, but was told that the instruments were ordered but were not here yet, or other excuses were given. One day he came and said that it was Ramadan, a Muslim holiday and he wanted an operation there and then. He just lay down on the couch and said he would not move till the operation was performed! Govind asked Dr. Sunil Bhatt, a friend of his who worked in the Provincial Hospital to assist, which he did.

The operation consisted of a large cut with the knife at the corneal periphery, and expressing the nucleus of the cataract with the two thumbs, and washing the remains of the cataract with an undine. The nucleus was removed, but there were problems washing the cataract, so old Bhatt was asked to blow through the tubing of the Undine, which he did, and it worked. The man had the pleasure of seeing for many years. Some years later, Govind was visiting his friend, the good doctor in Kenya, and he had the pleasure of performing surgery on this patient's other eye. He was a happy man for the remainder of his life.

CHAPTER 49

⋖ ❦0❧ ⋗

Mr. Mulji Devchand Shah

Mr. M. D. Shah ran a retail store in Nyeri. It so happened that his young daughter of about 11 yrs. had an accident with her glasses, with the result that the frame as well as the lenses had broken. Mr. shah came to the office and recounted the story about the accident and a need for a new pair for glasses for his daughter. She had an examination of her eyes, and was noted to have short sightedness of 3 Diopters. Mr. Shah was shown the kind of glasses that were commonly used for the African patients. They were circular lenses in wire frames, and functionally good but cosmetically poor. Mr. Shah was informed in no uncertain terms that his daughter will very likely not accept these, and a better pair should be ordered for her. Mr. Shah was somewhat miserly, however. He was told the glasses as shown to him would be 35 Shillings, although it was thought that she would not accept the cosmetically poor glasses, but he was only interested in them and wished these to be ordered. The unattractive glasses were ordered and these came in a few days.

Mr. Shah appeared the next day in the office crestfallen. He said that as soon as his daughter saw the glasses she threw them across the room and said that there was no way she was going to wear them. He wanted to return the glasses and a new pair of a better design be ordered. A phone call to Nairobi was made and he was told that it would cost 125 Shs for nicer glasses., to which he agreed. The glasses came and she was happy with them.

However, there was the cost of the old pair, which was nonrefundable. Even the Doctor could not return them to the suppliers. As the cost was 35 Shs., it was decided to split the difference, and he would be liable to hRodney of the cost, which was 17.50 Shs., to which he agreed. Govind had the advantage now of showing the pair that his daughter had rejected, to the people who would want to buy this type of glasses. Then the usual problem that is common among the Asians started. A bill was sent every month but it was ignored as long as possible. After several months he appeared in the office to pay the bill. Then he wants the bill reduced, although he was told that the profit margins were miDinual. But he maintained that the advantage was to Govind because now he had the frames to show the patients. Govind was quite angry, and brought the frames with lenses in front of him and broke them to pieces with his own hands, to prove that there was no advantage now. Drinker's hands were bleeding, and Mr. Shah felt bad and left. Anyone who has complaints against the good Doctor goes to the arbitrator, none other than Mr. Nanjibhai, his father, and tells of all the mistreatments from his son's hands. He eventually paid the bill with a reduced price. What a storm in a teacup!

CHAPTER 50

Harvinder Basan—a tragedy

Colonel Joseph Benchley was a retired farmer in the Mweiga area, which is about twenty miles from Nyeri. He was in the British Army, and on retirement the Government of the day had been kind to him and gave him several sections of land. He had done quite well as a result of his hard work. He was driving along on one of the minor roads in his old car, when he saw a man on the road. He looked wounded, so he stopped and wondered as to what had happened to him. The man's name was Mr. Basan who told him that his whole family was attacked by highway robbers, but he and his little daughter had survived the attack. There was a smashed up car on the side of the road. Just outside was the body of a woman, and besides her, the delicate body of a child. His daughter of about seven was also on the side of the road, crying. She had a small wound on her arm, as well as a large cut on the nose. He took Mr. Basan and the child to the Provincial Hospital in Nyeri. The two were put in a small ward assigned to Asians consisting of four beds and is some 100 Yards from the main Hospital. It was obvious that the little girl was frightened of her dad and cried anytime he approached her. Govind and Dinbala took them some flowers, and sat by the bedside for a while. Mr. Basan was quiet all the time, and appeared to be brooding. This was regarded as being due to the mental anguish he was going through. The bodies of his wife and child were brought to Hospital. His wife had died from multiple wounds inflicted by a Panga, a type of Machete used in Kenya. She was hit 35 times with it! The child was also fatally wounded.

The Asian Community in Nyeri, whose President was a Dr. Madhoke, were up in arms. Africans were blamed, and it was demanded by the community that all Asians should be allowed to carry a firearm on their person. It really riled the Africans, and since that day, Dr. Madhoke's practice tumbled and never recovered from it.

The police unraveled the story eventually. It appeared that it was all Mr. Basan's doing. He had fallen in love with a lady who worked as a nurse at Kenyatta Hospital in Nairobi. As a consequence, he wanted to get rid of his family, and had hired two murderers for the grisly crime. He used to take his family for country rides, and have these characters waiting for them. Eventually they saw their chance and carried out the heinous act. He had told them to hit him in the arm with the blunt end of the Panga as well so that the story would become plausible. The Africans were caught and confessed to everything. There was a trial of the three culprits at the Law Courts in Nyeri. They were all found guilty and hanged.

CHAPTER 51

❬❧◦❧❭

Dinu resumes studies in England

After giving birth to Sheila, a beautiful daughter, Dinbala was getting restless. She came to the office daily but her heart was not there. She expressed a desire to go to England, and resume her studies and complete her course in Nursing. A ticket was bought for her and she departed for England. She was readmitted at Broadgreen Hospital in Liverpool, and resumed studies from where she had left off. She eventually completed her course with brilliance, and the family was reunited again some years later. There was no problem for looking after Sheila, the daughter, as the ever present and loving grandma was there. Grandma had never gone to school, but her store of knowledge was vast, and with a tender heart she would recount all the stories of Rama and Krishna; She was full of sayings for all occasions and her wisdom was like an ocean, never ending, ever nurturing.

Sheila was a stout beautiful girl that everyone loved. She had her own lingo, and loved her soothers. She loved them so much that she had one tied around her neck, one tied to each wrist, and still always had a few more nearby. One evening, grandma was talking to her and said: 'Sheila, you are a big girl now. You should give up your 'buchis' (Soothers).

'Yes grandma, you are right', says the little princess. So she throws away her soothers over the high wall that surrounds the house onto some mud and grass. Midnight came, and she wants the buchi. The whole family was outside with torches in hands, looking for them. It was a comical site.

Many a time, Govind came home after the day's work, around 4 p.m. and collect Sheila and drive in his Mercedes 190, colored red, and later a blue one, Mercedes 220S, around the Tetu Hills and many villages in the area that dotted the country side.

❬❧◦❧❭

CHAPTER 52

Lucy the Monkey

Govind bought a small monkey and brought it home. It was a macaque monkey, with bright starry eyes and appeared to be quite friendly. The family named her Lucy. As Lucy grew, she had a belt put around her lower waist, to which a leash could be tied. It was interesting to see Sheila taking the monkey for a walk, when in fact it was the monkey that was pulling on the leash. Then Govind acquired two cats, and called one of them 'Manju' in memory of a long lost girlfriend. In memory of her, Manju had all forms of jewelry around her neck. It was interesting to see the monkey giving the cats a hard time, and it was all recorded on film.

It was impossible to manage the monkey in the courtyard where she was tied. The place became dirty, and Nanjibhai felt that the monkey should be moved to the back of the house, and that was done. Unfortunately, she was tied at the back behind the two toilets. It was disconcerting for anyone that went to the toilet, that as soon as one set down on the throne then a face would appear on the back window, peering down at the person's bodily functions. The curious face was that of Lucy.

She was on a fairly long leash, and she did not seem to like black people, many of whom came to sell their wares like vegetables etc. She would quietly but quite rapidly run to them and bite them at their ankles!

Some years later, Govind left Kenya, and Nanjibhai took the monkey out in the jungles, at a distance of about twenty miles, but that did not make any difference, as she just found her way back. Amazing! She was eventually sold off to a Somali resident in the town.

CHAPTER 53

❰ ❥๐๏ ❱

An unsinkable boat

At one time Govind took a notion that he would like to own a boat. He found an undiscovered pristine lake that was just beautiful. The lake was pristine, and luckily access to it was not difficult. He would visit there with his daughter, and whenever he visited, he would see a particular old woman who would come every day, and sit by the lake. She was totally naked and covered with ashes, some of which was vertically striped on her body. She would build a fire and cook with a small pot. She would then enjoy her supper, and wash her pot in the lake and depart for home—wherever that was.

Govind formed the concept of a boat, and started to gather all the discarded boxes that were a reject from many stores. He would come home at lunchtime and in the evenings, and work on the project. He would cut, and nail all the pieces together. This went on for some months. He worked on it continuously even though many thought and said that it would never float. In fact Nanjibhai said that he would become Govind's slave if it ever floated. The construction was completed and was taken out to the lake and it floated quite well, considering all the strange materials that went into its construction.

The boat was then covered with discarded rubberized airplane material, which made it waterproof. Unfortunately, the boat became rather heavy. A very kind man called Babu Shah offered his truck so that the boat could be taken to the lake. The offer was accepted with pleasure. It was taken and put on ground by the lake. It took about four men to bring it down. Then it was pushed on the water. It went quite well, and was moved along with a couple of oars that were also cut from some wood. The boat leaked, but the wood was rather heavy, with a base of about three layers, all of which helped to float it quite well. Unfortunately it was too heavy to take home, and was left on the lake. Many Africans behaved as though it belonged to their nonexistent navy and had a lot of fun with it. Eventually they broke it up and used it for firewood. After this his younger brother went to an auction in Nairobi and bought a proper boat, in which the family had a lot of fun. Many visitors who had come to see the family also enjoyed an afternoon trip on the boat.

There was an old woman that used to come and sit by the lake all day, every day. She was totally in the nude, and smeared with ashes. She used to cook by the lake. She had all the requirements with her. She mumbled a lot. After her day's picnic, she collected her worldly supplies, and after a good cleanup with the lake water, she walked away into the jungle.

CHAPTER 54

Mr. Matusia Mazioki

Matusia was a pleasant and a humble man. He worked hard as he had to support two wives and several children. Unfortunately he also had asthma, and would come about once a month to Govind's office for an injection of Adrenaline for relief. He came one day and the nurse gave the said injection. He presented himself at Govind's home early morning the next day saying that the area of the injection site was swollen. Indeed it was swollen and firm, affecting the outer aspect of the thigh where the injection was given. As no definite diagnosis could be made, he was taken to the Hospital where he was admitted and antibiotics were given. Unfortunately he got no better, and on the next day he collapsed and died, despite heroic measures by the doctors and nurses that worked there. A postmortem was performed, and it was noted that the whole leg had gas gangrene, which is caused by a germ called 'Clostridium Welchii'. Gas can be felt under the skin, as crepitating if one knows what they are looking for, and the wound has to be opened out and exposed to air. It was a tragic case, but it could not be ascertained as to what could have caused it—there were unproven theories, one was that the nurse had just been the washroom before giving the injection, and her hygiene was questioned. The injection was made in India, and that also come under suspicion, as there had been an example when at one time a doctor who was preparing an injection with a solution that had a fly in it! The solution was prepared and made in India.

CHAPTER 55

A child that had collapsed

Mr. Jentibhai Pankhania came to the office one day. He said that the Doctor should come urgently as his child at home had collapsed. Some of the patients who were urgent and had priority were seen, and the Doctor went with him with his bag that had all the emergency supply needed. He saw that there was a dead child in his mother's lap. She said that the child had just collapsed without any reason about an hour ago. The child was in the kitchen at the time, and there were quite a few raw peas on the floor. Resuscitative measures were tried, including an injection of adrenaline into the heart without avail. The child's body was transferred to the hospital for a postmortem. At the autopsy it was found that the child's trachea had a pea that had obstructed his breathing. The story became clearer, and it would appear that he was eating raw peas, as there were a few in his hands when he collapsed. It also seemed that as he had a small tiff with his mother he was pouting and it happened that he sucked heavily, and the pea that was in his mouth was pulled into the trachea, and blocked it. A thump given immediately on his back would have cleared the problem, but unfortunately a life was lost needlessly.

CHAPTER 56

A child with Malaria

One day a child was brought to the office, with a story that the child had been quite healthy till recently when the child had recurrent fever. A diagnosis of malaria was made, and a quarter of a cc. of chloroquine, made by a famous outlet in Britain, was given. The child was then allowed to go, but in about hRodney an hour the child was brought back, as the child had started to have fits. Despite efforts to save the child, it was not successful. It was not clear as to why there was a reaction to the drug, and enquiry with the manufacture reassured the Doctor that the drug was completely safe. It may have been that the nurse was a little heavy handed when she gave the injection.

CHAPTER 57

A Bleeder

An African woman had just visited the market and was leaving. As she left, she fell onto a piece of glass, which cut her hand for about on inch. The cut was on the palm near the thumb. It was bleeding copiously.

Numerous clamps were applied, and there was no time to give a local anesthetic. The vessel was eventually clamped saving the woman ensanguining herself and losing her life.

CHAPTER 58

Mr. Josaiah Kariuki Mwangi

Mr. Mwangi was a politician. He was a friendly person, somewhat tall, with impressive features—long face, well shaven, expressive mouth with prominent lips, and very intense in whatever he was talking about. He belonged to the K.A.N.U. (Kenya African National Union) party, the only political party existent at the time in Kenya, and was its secretary. He had also been a prisoner in a British Camp as he was suspected of taking part in the Mau Mau, which was a violent movement to gain independence from Britain.

He had in fact written a book about his experiences while in the camp, and called it 'Behind Barbed Wire Fences'. He was active in obtaining the release of Jomo Kenyatta, who became the first President of Kenya on his release from Prison. Eventually he became the secretary to the party, and it was thought that he would take over as President when President Kenyatta steps down. Unfortunately he suffered bad dreams after release from jail, and was convinced that only an injection of Penicillin given as at that time would cure the disease. He presented to Govind's office for the procedure occasionally, and wished for Govind to join the party and take an active interest. Unfortunately, neither he nor any other Asian (apart from one or two people) joined the party, as they were all busy serving their Goddess Laxmi, which, as you know is the Goddess of wealth.

The story has a sad ending. At that time it was said that any man that was a threat to the powers that be was eliminated, (e.g. Tom Mboya) and Mr. Mwangi was no exception. He was found hanging from a tree outside Nairobi one morning.

CHAPTER 59

◄❧o❧►

Matatus of Kenya and Tulsi

Do you know what a Matatu is? A Matatu is a passenger bus that is nothing but a deathtrap. It is crammed with passengers like sardines, some of whom are almost hanging out, as there is no room to sit in the bus. Of course, there are no seat belts. The bus is poorly maintained, with the tires that are almost flat from wear. The brakes can fail at any time, and are not maintained at all. The driver is generally a maniac who has been given a carte blanche with regard to the speed at which he can drive, or the manner in which he can drive. He can overtake wherever he wants, even if it is dangerous to do so, and with total disregard to regulations or road conditions. Of course, for the owners it can be a good money making machine.

Over 3,000 people a year die in traffic in Kenya, mostly from the missiles called Matatus. However, to be fair, the Government of today is trying to bring in strict regulations that will improve the situation.

At one time Tulsi along with his parents was returning from Nairobi. They reached Ragati Hill, a hill that is about eight miles long, and is uphill all the way. Tulsi was the driver of the Mercedes. They were deep in conversation, when they saw a Matatu rearing down the hill towards them. The tire on the Matatu was worn and burst while the bus was at high speed. The driver had difficulty controlling the vehicle, and it swerved into the path of the Mercedes. A collision was unavoidable. There was a head on crash. Six of the passengers in the Matatu were flung out and died immediately. The crash of metal against metal brought along a horrendous roar and of course a total and immediate mangling of the two vehicles. The passengers of the Mercedes were not spared either. Tumutumu Hospital was nearby and the injured were taken there. Nanjibhai and his wife Jamkur got away with minor injuries. Despite heroic measures, they were unable to revive Tulsi. Tulsi was cremated in Nyeri. He left behind a grieving widow, and three children.

◄❧o❧►

CHAPTER 60

Govind's abysmal depression

It was a day no different than any other day. It was bright and sunny in the morning, but in the afternoon it became dull, with cloudy skies that totally blanketed the sun. Later on it started to rain. The rain slowly increased to a torrent by suppertime, which went well into the evening and into the night. The corrugated metal roof emanated its own music with the pitter-patter of the rain. It was not raining cats and dogs but elephants and rhinos!

Govind started to reminisce about his life in Kenya, and the future that was ahead. He had a daughter that was under the care of his mother, while his wife was overseas continuing his studies. His practice was going steady, but there was not much money to be made. All the money was given to the store without even a thank you. Expressing a desire that one of the buildings should be transferred met with a negative response. His Sinus problem was getting worse with continuous discharge that was becoming bloody lately. An operation by Dr. Pramukh Patel in the form of Sinus drainage and straightening out of the deviated septum in the nose was not much of a success. The depression deepened and became overwhelming. Govind cried and cried. The family gathered all around and tried to console him, but without avail. That was when he made the decision to leave his practice in Nyeri and go to Britain and gather his family with him once again. Since that day, as a memory, he started to wear his watch on the right hand.

CHAPTER 61

❮❧❀❦❯

Dr. Sunil Bhatt

Dr. Sunil Bhatt was the resident gynecologist at the Provincial Hospital. His wife, Anita was also a resident Doctor at the local Hospital. A friendship developed amongst them. Their internships were to expire soon. Govind told them about his plan to leave the country and wondered if the couple would be interested in taking over the practice. They eventually confirmed with Govind that they would indeed take over the practice. Money was not discussed, and learning that finances were not discussed was quite upsetting to Mr.Nanjibhai, but he could not do much about it. The practice included the pharmacy, many instruments, furniture, the staff, as well as all the patients. He had also acquired many dental instruments over the years. It certainly was a good deal for the couple.

Plans went ahead for Govind to leave and go to Britain. He sold his car, and gave more money on top so that he would get a new car supplied by the same company in Britain. Jamnadas made a contribution towards it.

Govind approached his father and asked him to contribute money so that more of drugs can be bought, and Govind and Sunil would give free service to the public, and that way Sunil would become known to all the people. The plan was carried out, and on the first day it went well, and the two saw a large number of patients. The news spread like wildfire, and the next day there was a long queue of people about a mile long outside the office. The police had to be called in to manage the crowd. All examinations and treatments were given, but the practice was discontinued on the day after due to an overwhelming response. Mrs. Festus was fired as she was found to have drugs from the office in her coat pocket. It is possible that Papdo might have placed the drugs there, as he did not like her.

Sunil Bhatt took over the practice, and the two made a fantastic success of it. Another colleague of his who specialized in Ear Nose and Throat joined them. As a courtesy, the two continued to look after Govind's parents and their families at no charge.

The two eventually left the country and now reside in Galveston, Texas, where the lady had an uncle who had invited them to his town and join the health services there.

RETURN
TO
ENGLAND

CHAPTER 62

⟨఼ 0ಌ ⟩

Return to England

A New Beginning

Sunil took over the Medical Practice in Nyeri, and Govind departed for England, along with his daughter Sheila, and his mother Jamkurben. The latter had bought a ticket to stay in England for six months. Going to England felt like returning home. He also had confidence that the advanced country would cure him permanently of his sinus problems.

On arrival at Heathrow Airport, they were met by Dinbala, and after the usual hugs and kisses, the family decided to go to Brighton where Dinu's younger sister Chandri lived before heading for the home city of Liverpool.

They took the train to Victoria Station, and changed the train there to go to Brighton. As they settled in the coach, there was a strong smell of pickles. Pickled mangoes, limes etc. are good to eat, but they can smell bad. The cause of the smell was located in Zaverben's cloth bag that she was carrying with her. It appears that she was dragging a jar of pickles in it that was leaking all the way from the Airport, to the station, and then in the train to Brighton—drip, drip, drip, the oily concoction dripped! The compartment was cleaned up rather hastily in the best way possible before English people came in wondering if these new immigrants were weird in some ways.

Chandri was a student of Art, and was doing quite well at the Brighton School of Fine Arts in Brighton. She had a basement apartment, but being artistic, and flamboyant, and because she liked the color pink, she had painted everything pink in her apartment, and that included everything, including the television, walls, her bed etc.

Chandri did well in Art School, but unfortunately she put on some weight and became a smoker. She had an aneurysm in the head that burst. She managed to survive after an operation that repaired the aneurysm. Chandri eventually died in her apartment. She was alone at the time, and it took days for anyone to become concerned about her absence. When it was noticed that she had not emerged from her apartment for some time, the police were called to break the door open to get to her.

She was a smart lady who really cared for the environment. She had a daughter of her own, and adopted a child when they were in New Zealand where they had immigrated for a few years.

In Liverpool, Govind's brother, Maganlal met them; (He was a student in the Law School in the University at the time).He had arranged accommodations near Walton Hospital, about 4 Miles out going east. Unfortunately, it was also near a prison, which formed a cloud of concern in the family's mind. The owner of the house, a Mrs. Bryson, had gone for a year to stay with her sister in Florida, and a lease was signed so that the house could be rented for a year. Life began anew, and Sheila started school. There was a neighbor, a Mrs. Carrington, who had seven daughters. Sheila played with the children there, so much so that if anyone asked as to whom she was, she said that she was 'Sheila Carrington'!

Dinbala was already working at Broadgreen Hospital, and it was left for Govind to hunt for a job. He applied at Alderhey Children's Hospital and was accepted there to work as a Senior House Officer. He was to do six months of Casualty work and six months of Surgical work. Alderhey was the largest Children's Hospital in the British Empire, boasting of over 1500 Beds. The Medical Superintendent was a Dr. Smithells—a very astute, sympathetic and well-read gentleman.

Casualties were like many others throughout the world. Children, who are sick from various diseases, swallowing poisons that the parents did not put them out of reach, abuse with cuts and bruises etc. The place was a bedlam at times. The Sisters that were in charge of the Department were like sergeant majors, and some did not have any sympathies for either the child or the parents. They tended to be quite rough with the children, a result of the same kind of repetitive work that one becomes numb to eventually.

Surgical work was something else. Govind worked for a Mr. Peter Paul Rickham, or PP as he was often called. He was a megalomaniac. His surgical lists started at 8 a.m. and went onto well at night. Govind and his Senior Registrar were to help him with the surgeries, ward rounds etc. He also specialized in the treatment of hydrocephalus, and the department was responsible for admitting all the children from the area as well as North Wales. Many children, who were born with Spina Bifida. It was not known that it was the lack of a Vitamin, Folic Acid, which if taken by the mother during her pregnancy would have prevented this form of havoc. Children have parts of the skull that are not fused, and fluid is removed by inserting a needle into the ventricles of the brain. PP had developed what was a called a 'Rickham's Button', which was the swollen end of a tube under the skin, the other end of the tube was inserted into the ventricle of the Brain. Thus a needle would have to just under the skin, and one had to remove about 40 c.c.s of Cerebrospinal fluid daily! There were about eight or nine patients to be drained every morning, before the normal surgical list started, hence work would have to start at 6 or 7 in the morning. Some patients had the Spitz Holter Valve inserted. The system was to drain the extra fluid into the heart or the peritoneal cavity. Unfortunately, many of these blocked or got infected. It was the responsibility of a Mr. Penn, who was from Australia, to attend to all these cases. It was not unknown to hear him talk to distraught parents and consoling them at 2 in the morning. He was bleary eyed in the morning, and often had his own lists or take over his boss's surgical list when he was not available. There were no holidays for anyone to be had, and at one time Govind had asked for and obtained a weekend's permission to go and see his sister in law in Brighton, but on his return he was severely reprimanded! The job also included visits to Olive Mount Children's Hospital, where children who needed chronic care were admitted. Children who had E.Coli infections and had to be isolated, children who became retarded because of Phenyketonuria (prevented now by dietary means), etc. It was a very busy job for the year. Alderhey Children's Hospital came in the news recently when a pathologist had started removing organs from children who had passed away without parental consent. He was sent packing to his country of origin.

CHAPTER 63

A Navy blue Ford Cortina

Govind sold his car, which was a Mercedes, in Kenya, and paid extra money on top so that he could get a new car in Britain. He had negotiated for a red car, an automatic, with a through front seat. He was assured that he would get this. Little did he know that the Brits did not even know what an automatic car is! In England, he was told that a car was not available, as the factory in Dagenham had closed down for the season. After about two week he got a phone call from the Ford Company in London that there was a car available; it was navy blue, 4 Door but had no other features that Govind had paid for. Since there was no choice, Govind took the train down, and he was given the car. He was not given instructions as to the different aspects of the car, but it was easy to learn, and a pleasure to drive in the ensuing years. However, it gave a lot of concern as it would stop at traffic lights etc. and it was difficult to get the donkey going again. Then there was the battery, for some reason it was always down, and the car had to be pushed to get it started! Thus, apart from the driver, it was always necessary to have a kind passenger in the car whose services would be needed whenever the car needed to be started. Generally the helper was his wife or his brother.

CHAPTER 64

Mrs. Bryson and Notice

T he owner of the house came back from Florida in about three months—much earlier than planned (the lease was for one year). She visited the house, and saw some remodeled and put together furniture around. These parts of furniture Govind had found in the coal shed, and had repaired them by assembling appropriate sections and making them usable once again. She also noted that Dinu would visit the Laundromat rather than wash the clothes at home. So she went to a lawyer, claiming that her house was wrecked, including the furniture. She had herself seen the lady of the house going to the Laundromat because she had broken her washing machine. She was a mean lady and the family had to vacate in a month's time. A hunt for another place of residence was started.

CHAPTER 65

A Watery Mess

One evening Govind came home to find that Sheila and her grandma were removing buckets of water from the upstairs toilet, running downstairs with them, emptying them in the sink, then back again. They were exhausted. It appeared that someone had gone to the toilet, and then had pulled the chain. However, the water did not stop running but continued to flow continuously and incessantly, and the two did not know what to do. It was overflowing! There was water flowing down the steps and towards the living room. They were panic stricken and exhausted. All one had to do was to pull the chain again and the water would stop. It was done and the water stopped to flow. Then came the cleanup, and only after that the family could relax.

CHAPTER 66

Move of residence once again

Following on to Mrs. Bryson's notice to vacate, a hunt for a new place of residence started. The British are very subtle in their color bar, although they may appear to be friendly and above board. The fact is realized when one is looking for a job etc. Many a Doctor is in fact was stuck in junior positions because of the prejudice.

The family located a house that was for sale by the owner, a Mr. Hasty, for two and a half thousand pounds. It was on 466 Queens Drive. It was a beautiful house, with high ceilings. The front room was large, and along the front bay window was built storage space, which was extensive. Behind it was a 'morning room', and then the kitchen, and behind it a garage. Upstairs was the master bedroom, a small room, and another bedroom. Further up was the attic, which in fact was a bedroom, albeit the ceiling was somewhat low, as it was sloping, to go along with the line of the roof.

There was the usual problem of finances. Govind wrote a letter to his dad in Nyeri about it, but Nanjibhai's reply was rather scathing, saying that not only was there was no money in Govind's name, but in fact he never made any money, and he was a burden at home in Kenya. He was also told that he spent more money than what he brought home. (It was obvious some years later that in fact there was a large amount of money deposited for Govind from his income, and was declared to the Government every year as such. He was never told about this!) It was obvious that any money coming from that source was not possible. His father in law, Damjibhai heard about the family's dilemma, and sent a check for two thousand pounds. Dinbala did not feel that that money should be used, so the check was returned, but then again, Damjibhai would not hear of it, so he sent the check back. As goodwill gesture Govind kept it but it was not used personally; but was used for his family members who had come to Britain in the coming years for further studies. Overtures were made with the British Medical Association, and an Insured loan for the amount was obtained. The family moved into this grand residence. However, it was not realized that Queen's Drive, being the major thoroughfare about seven miles long, was noisy.

There was also a bus stop right in front of the house, so the noises started at three in the morning and went on till about midnight. However, it is remarkable how much the human organism can adapt, and after about a week, all the noise and bustle was not a problem. At the west end was Penny Lane, made famous by the Beatles in their music. In fact the club where they used to sing was close to the eye hospital.

CHAPTER 67

Mr. Hopkins

Govind came across Mr. Hopkins at Alderhey Hospital. Govind often visited the Eye Clinic at the Hospital although he was not required to do so. Mr. Hopkins was the consultant in charge of the Eye Department at the Hospital. The two liked each other immediately, and it continued close to friendship for many years. He became his mentor and channeled his life in the right direction.

He was a tall and burly gentleman, very typically British. He was hard working, bright, sincere and helpful. He had a monocle in front of his left eye, which gave him somewhat of a comical appearance. A light green woolen thread was hanging from the monocle, the other end of which went into his coat. One could see and hear him dictating letters to his secretary for hours after a very busy eye clinic. He enjoyed cataract surgery, which in those days was rather primitive. One did a section with a knife, the so called von Graefe knife, and pulled out the cataract, which of course is the lens in the eye that has gone opaque, with a pair of forceps specially designed for it. The wound then was closed, but no sutures were used, hoping that nature will do the rest of the requirements by the eye to heal. If nature did not blind the patient, then surgery certainly did, as the lens of the eye that does the focusing was removed. The situation was improved with glasses that were as thick as the bottom part of a coke bottle! He took a liking for Govind, and whenever Govind was looking for a new job, if Mr. Hopkins was part of the interviewing team, then he was sure he would get the job!

There were many cataracts to be done in Clatterbridge Hospital. However, in the afternoon he would get restless and wished to go home. Govind took over the list and had the pleasure of completing the day's list. He gained a lot of experience and expertise in performing cataract surgeries.

CHAPTER 68

466 Queens Drive; Home at last

The family moved into the house and had nothing but happy memories while they were there, which was for many years. Many a friend of the family came for a visit, enjoyed the food, as well the heaters that warmed the body and souls, especially coming in from the cold and of course the company. Maganlal took the attic room upstairs, and Sheila took one of the rooms on the second floor. Kashiben, Govind's mother in law came over and stayed for six months. She enjoyed the Television very much, and had the habit of sitting in front of it but also twirling her rosary in her hands at the same time. It was hard to know what she was concentrating on, as if there was something in the television that she would not understand then she would ask anyone present as to what was said. She always wore beautiful Saris. It should be realized that a person with a Sari was a rare person in those days in Britain, and if she went out for a walk, she would attract a number of dogs that would follow her, as they could not fathom this curious creature.

There was a time when Sheila attended the kindergarten at Allenby Square. One had to go along the West Derby Lane, cross a major road with traffic lights, and reach the nursery. One day she volunteered to go and collect Sheila from the nursery. She was given permission to go. On the way a number of dogs followed her as was their habit of following any strangers, specially the one that dressed differently, like a sari etc. She had no problem finding the place. She collected the little girl, and started for home. Disaster! She could not find her way back! Evening was drawing nigh, and panic set in. She went this way and that without avail. A nice man in a car pulled up, and asked her what the problem was. She made him understand the problem. He then took the couple to various roads, and different houses. There was relief when she found the right house and swore that she would never do it again!

CHAPTER 69

◄ ❧ o ❧ ►

Anita, another star is born

Dinbala was pregnant, and went to see her family doctor, who was called Doctor Kennedy. The doctor was Irish, and one could smell alcohol on in his breath. If Dinu or Govind came to his office, he would get off his chair, and give it to the visiting doctor or his wife! At the mention of any illness, he would ask what Govind thought of it, and what the treatment should be. Nearer the end of her term, Dinbala started having pains, so she went to see the good doctor. He asked the usual questions, and Govind was called on the phone at the Eye Hospital for advice. Govind said that she should be given an injection of Pethidine (Demerol) to control the pains, and be referred to the Hospital, the nearest one serving the area was Sefton General Hospital. After some delay, the Ambulance came and took her to the Hospital. The casualty Department was all prepared as they were told that there was a very important personality coming in the ambulance. She was taken to the casualty Dept. Govind heard the news and drove home, only to be told that the ambulance had taken her to the Hospital. He was panic stricken, and rushed to the Hospital in his car. A junior officer had examined her who afterwards had an interview with Govind, and told him that he should realize that his wife was going to lose the baby. Govind was mad at that and told him that he should make sure she does not lose the baby, and the pains should be stopped by an injection of Pethidine, as this was not given yet. She was admitted in a ward, and after settling down, she was given the injection, at three in the morning! After a week or so she was released to recuperate at home.

Deliveries in Britain are mostly done at home. Once nature gives notice that a a woman will be going into labor, the midwife and her assistant come over and stay put until the baby is delivered. They are served with tea and cookies as long as necessary. They are motherly women who have seen drama of life quite often and deal with them quite efficiently. They are also in touch with the family Doctor, who is summoned if necessary. A 'Flying Squad' would come if a disaster was thought to be imminent.

It was about three in the morning, January 09, 65 that this bright spark was born. Soon after delivery, Govind went around the house telling all that a girl was born, and that now they can sleep in peace till the morning.

Anita grew up as a bright and beautiful child. Wide black circles set in a small face with black curly hair. She knew her nursery rhymes completely by the time she was two, and she often just rolled on the floor as she recited them. It was remarkable when she was put on the potty, as her feet could not touch the floor, but moved in rhythm as she sang her nursery rhymes, and when she was done, she departed from the potty but left quite an impression on the large amount of clay that was left behind.

She was not very fussy at night and generally slept well. However, Govind had made up a contraption, which consisted of tying a string from the ceiling, and then tying a milk bottle at the other end, so that the little girl should take a sip whenever she felt like it! It worked wonderfully well.

One day it was rather interesting. The long coils in a heater were rusting and breaking up. Govind just got a new coil, and started to remove the old one, which came out in pieces. Little Anita decided to give him company. Govind did not realize that as he putting down the pieces of the coil, she was helping herself, and having a good feed. By the time Govind's brilliant job was done, Anita had a good fill too! She came to few painful days afterwards, but no harm was done.

She grew up in Canada, became an R.N. but later realized that her calling was different, so she went off to McGill University in Montreal to learn the Piano, and obtained her degree in her calling. She is now a Piano teacher. She married a man called Mr. Robert Bilton who has a welding firm in the nearby town of Slave Lake. They have four bright children. The welding firm has become a success beyond imagination.

CHAPTER 70

◄ ❧0❧ ►

Saint Paul's Eye Hospital

The year at the Children's Hospital was coming to an end for Govind. He had tried the D.C.H. (Diploma in child health) without success. He did not have a great desire to continue treating children. However, the job for Registrar in the Hospital was advertised, and Govind applied, and was reassured that he would get the job if he presented himself for the interview. It was to take place in the coming week. It was a disappointment to all concerned when Govind did not present himself at the interview for a job in the Children's Hospital. Govind had attended occasionally in the Ophthalmology Department's Eye Clinics, and he had seen many interesting cases there. He also came across a nice man called Mr. Bill Hopkins. He had a chat with with him regards to his future. He was told that he should take up Ophthalmology, and if he wanted, interviews for the job were being held at the Eye Hospital the next day and he could be recommended for the job by him. There were a number of candidates to be interviewed at the Hospital the next day, but as Govind was a graduate of Liverpool University, he knew he would be given a priority. The next day he went to the interview, and was accepted for the job as a Senior House Officer in Ophthalmology. The job consisted in rotating every three months in the various departments in consisting of Medicine, Surgery, Casualties etc. and under different consultants.

The Eye Hospital was at the end of Tithebarn Street. (The hospital is gone, and a major highway runs through it now). It was a very busy hospital, and patients quite often came with their own sandwiches as a wait of five or six hours to see a doctor was not uncommon. All forms of eye injuries, and other ocular diseases were seen. Some were bad and advanced, as when a woman with a ruptured eye presented with a history that she was walking along a golf course, when she was hit in her eye with a golf ball. The eye was a mess, and the lens of the eye was lying on her shoulder! All forms of injuries had to be repaired, and metal foreign bodies were removed, often with the giant magnet that pulled out the foreign body. Bits of metal, if left in the eye start to rust rapidly as there is a current going through the eye continuously. Detached Retinas had to be repaired urgently. Cataracts removed, corneal grafts performed etc. There were cases of tumors of all kinds—the devastating retinoblastomas of childhood, which present as a white reflex in the pupil were treated, but unfortunately many are present in both the eyes on first presentation. Adult tumors commonly called melanomas were also seen. The eye has to be removed if the person's life was to be saved; even then it was often quite late with the result that the patient did not survive and died from the devastation caused by the tumor. These tumors later spread seedlings and grew in the liver, bones etc. They were not even radiosensitive so radiotherapy was useless for these tumors.

The consultants were fantastic and good teachers. At one time Govind had to work for a consultant called Mr. Edwin Cook, who took a liking for him. A Dr. Chowdhery, who was Govind's registrar, had to call Mr. Cook now and then at home, whenever there was an emergency. Mr. Cook would enquire as to what Govind thought of the problem, and would even ask Govind to perform the surgery, which was rather embarrassing, as Dr. Chowdhery was the Registrar and senior to him. Mr. Cook was a heavy smoker, and paid a price because of the transgression. He had cancer of the lung and died from it.

CHAPTER 71

◄ ৯ o ৶ ►

Sinus problems

The Sinus problems along with Asthma that Govind had was getting worse. He knew the Orthopedic Surgeon called Mr. McFarland, and he knew a consultant also by the same name who was his brother. He thought he would go and see the said gentleman. He called him on the phone, and was advised to come and see him at Broadgreen Hospital on the next day at 10 in the morning. He presented himself on the day at his Out Patient Clinic, where he waited about an hour, when he was told that he should have his Sinuses X-Rayed first, so he went to the X-Ray Department and had his Sinuses X-Rayed, and took his films to the ENT Clinic, only to learn that the great man had left, and if Govind still wanted to see him then he should come to the ENT Hospital on the next day. So Govind went to the other Hospital along with the X-Rays of his Sinuses on the next day as told. He was told to wait in a room, where he patiently waited for two hours. The great man then presents himself, along with his entourage of Senior Registrar, students and nurses. He asked Govind as to what the problem was. Govind explained about his Sinuses, so he thought he would have a look. Then he agreed and thought that there was not much room to breathe for Govind, to which Govind agreed wholeheartedly. 'So, what do you want me to do for you?' said he. 'You do whatever is necessary', said Govind. 'Oh I am sorry', said he, 'I am away on holidays for a couple of months'. 'Perhaps I will ask Mr. Lorenz, my senior Registrar to take over the case'. So the other great man, Mr. Lorenz, an emigrant from Ceylon, looked at it and agreed that the Sinuses should be treated and he would take over the case. He booked Govind for the necessary surgical procedures. The day finally came for the surgery and Govind was admitted in the Hospital. AT night about 9 p.m. Mr. Lorenz did his rounds and came into Govind's room. He came along with the night sister. He was asked if he was comfortable, and if he wished for anything. 'Things are fine', said Govind, 'However I will have trouble getting to sleep at night'. So Mr. Lorenz ordered sleeping tablets for him. 10 O'clock came and no sight of the great sister, so Govind rang the bell, and she came and asked what the problem was.

Govind enquired again about the sleeping tablets. She said she would look into it. Nothing happened. It was 11 p.m. and Govind called again and the story was repeated. Midnight came and Govind called again. This time she came barging in, and gave Govind a reprimand. 'Just who do you think you are, calling for sleeping tablets all the time. Do you think I have nothing else to do?' and she banged the door and left. Govind was furious, and got ready to leave. A phone call was made home to come and collect him, when Dinu told him to calm down and take it easy. So he calmed down and stayed.

The surgery was performed on the next day in the form of an 'Antrostomy, on each side in the nose, i.e. making new permanent holes for the sinuses so they drain better, and 'submucus resection' i.e. removing the cartilage that is in the septum of the nose. Next day Dr. Lorenz decided to wash the sinuses, and he carried out the procedure. Govind had a bout of sneezing, which made the great Doctor mad, and he said he would never wash his sinuses again! It is obvious that in the medical and allied professions, the providers of caring health care, become heartless and apt lose their humanity if they are not constantly vigilant. It can also be argued that Govind did not make the best of patients. The operation helped some over the years, but in the process the tear duct was ruined, so the left eye watered heavily whenever Govind had a cough, sneeze etc.

CHAPTER 72

❨ৡ৹ঀ❩

Improvements at 466

It is not very wise to carry out any renovations etc with one's spouse, as each one has a different idea as to how to approach and carry out a particular renovation. Wallpapering the little room in pink wallpaper was not much of a problem, except when Govind had the bright idea of applying the glue directly on the wall—a disaster as the wallpaper was full of air bubbles. Govind covered the floor in Anita's room with square pieces of lino, and made a large star of the same material in the center. It worked out quite well and he was proud it.

Damjibhai, his father in law was visiting at one time, and the two decided to redo the floor in the kitchen. Things were going well, but one end of a square piece would not line up properly, so Govind had the bright idea of nailing the edge down. He told Damjibhai to apply a small nail at the edge, which he did. Disaster! He hit the main water pipe that was leading to the sink in the kitchen. Water started to pour out, and he did not know what to do. Govind had a bright idea again—he told him to apply another nail to close the hole caused by the first nail—that was done, but the water just increased. A plumber had to be called who had to close with a 'key' the main pipe leading to the house and do the necessary repairs.

One day the garage door was tackled. The layout of the garage was odd, as it was lengthwise, running along the narrow street at the back. To get the car in the garage was tricky, as the car tended to be very close to the walls etc. The door was heavy to handle, even though it was in 4 sections. Govind saw some discarded metal cots from the children's ward at the hospital. They were on wheels. He just brought them home, and disjoined the parts, and nailed the part with wheels to the garage doors. The door opened and closed like a charm since then.

One of the neighbors was a Mr. Drummond, who made everyone mad, as he would come home everyday and polish his car. The car was shiny and clean, and always made everyone else's look bad.

Damjibhai was a pleasure to have in the house. He had come for six months, and was useful with many chores around the house. He loved to see wrestling on the Television and spent hours watching men bashing each other.

CHAPTER 73

Diploma in Ophthalmology

At the end of the year, Govind, along with his friends John Broderick and Marvin Leukonia took the examination of Diploma in Ophthalmology and passed the examination. It was held in London. The examiners were in fact the giants of Ophthalmology, like Sir. Stewart Duke Elder, Sorsby, Trevor Roper, Roper Hall, Jamieson Evans as well as many others. They are stars that shine in the bright galaxy of ophthalmology, probably permanently.

Sir Stewart Duke Elder has written more 37 Volumes on ophthalmology, each of a thousand pages, and Arnold Sorsby, another author, has written four volumes.

CHAPTER 74

End of SHO job at St. Paul's

The year at the Hospital went like the blink of an eye. Once again one has to apply for a job, be interviewed if considered suitable, thus going up the slow and painful ladder that is Britain's National Health Service. It is a clever way to obtain cheap labor for as long as possible.

Well, Govind did not apply for a job, as in the horizon he could see a number of big hurdles that lay ahead in the progress of his career. The uphill struggle included the dreaded Primary Fellowship Examination, with eventual final examination for the F.R.C.S., or the Fellowship of the College of Surgeons. The subjects for the examination for the 'Primary' were Anatomy, Physiology, and related subjects like Histology, Embryology, Pathology etc. He tried to study for this examination while Dinbala juggled the pittance that came in from her work, with which the family had to support two children and a household of residents and visitors.

CHAPTER 75

⟨ৡ০ঽ⟩

Dr. J. Merrick

Dr. Merrick hailed from the Emerald Isle (Ireland) and practiced in West Derby. He had a lovely daughter, and a wife with whom he had a tumultuous relationship. He himself suffered from asthma. Add to that was his belief that women should only come in the mornings to his surgery, while the working men, and only these men, should present themselves in the evening. If he saw a woman in the evening, he would shout and scream at them, which certainly did not help his asthma. House calls in Britain are common, and whenever he paid a housecall, it was the patient that helped him climb the stairs prior to him treating them! In his office there was not even a stethoscope, as he did not believe in it.

Govind started to do occasional locums for him. It was hard to diagnose the patients without a stethoscope, but it was managed. Most of the patients had come for a repeat of their prescriptions. When they obtained their concoctions from the pharmacy, if even the color of the solution was different from what they were used to, then they would become irate and call the Doctor's office. They were happy once the color of the medicine was changed to the right color.

Mrs. Ham was the secretary.

'Does the new Doctor examine?' asked many a patient of her. If the answer was affirmative, then they would go away as they did not want to undress and be examined by an unknown person, even if he was a doctor.

Mrs. Ham was very observant, and often looked out of the window in the front, and watched some of the patient come in. From her observation, she would tell the doctor which of the patients had to be sent to the hospital for admission, some of them urgently, as they were very sick and liable to die at home. Needless to say that her advice was always heeded.

It happened. Dr. Merrick's illness got the better him and he departed this world and went to the great beyond.

The office was on the point of closure. It was available if Govind wanted to continue it, but Govind declined the offer from the doctor's family to buy the practice, much to the disappointment of many patients etc.

⟨ৡ০ঽ⟩

CHAPTER 76

Raaj

Another child was delivered at 466. There was rejoicing as it was a boy. Many hours were spent in enjoying the antiques of this baby, and in fact, Govind recorded his crying, and made one and all listen to it, whether they liked it or not.

He was called Raaj. He grew up in England, and later in Canada where he ran his own company that was related to software and hardware related to computers.

CHAPTER 77

❖

Emergency Call Service

A Dr. Maxwell, who had a medical practice in the center of the town, started this much-needed service. It consisted in hiring doctors in whose cars were put a metal box, which in fact was a walkie-talkie. It was about a foot wide, and 5 inches thick, to be placed under the dash of the doctor's car. A microphone was attached to it, and with the help of it, contact with the headquarters was made, and maintained kept up almost continuously. The doctor is told via the slave driver to attend to a housecall, and report as soon as it was done, so that he could be sent to the next one. It was very busy, and the remuneration was five pounds for six hours. Even in those days it amounted to down and outright slavery! Unfortunately, the machine was hard on the battery, and it would run down. It made the engine impossible to start, and the car had to be pushed to get it started. Because of this problem, a passenger had to be taken along, and his services obtained in pushing the donkey of a car and get it going once again. Once again with the engeine started, it made it possible to go for the next call. Generally it was his brother or his wife who accompanied him for the purpose. The car was stationed far from where the call was, so the patient does not suspect that the doctor came in a car that would not even start.

Some very interesting cases were seen. Many of whom were treated at home, while some were sent to the hospital.

It was interesting in that if there was a call for a sick child to be seen, the doctor would go to the home, and saw the parents continued to watch television. They would not even move but tell the doctor to go upstairs where the sick child was. The doctor would then go into the child's room and carry on with the examination and treatment as necessary. It was odd that the parents never came up. It seemed that boob tube was more important to them.

The one call in particular was interesting. The doctor was told to go and see a sick person in a particular house. The husband came out to the front driveway and met the doctor there. He told the good doctor not to worry as his wife was cured and there was no need to go and see her. However, for various reasons, the doctor could not accept the proposal. He insisted in going inside the house and seeing her. He entered the house only to find that in fact his wife was dead!

All kinds of illnesses and tragedies were seen in the ensuing months, but basically Govind was biding time. However, it was impossible to concentrate on work while living at home where there were many distractions.

IRELAND

CHAPTER 78

❨ ❧0❧ ❩

IRELAND

Dublin

Dinbala booked Govind to follow a course at the Royal College of Surgeons in the city of Dublin, Ireland. It was a four-month's course, after which the examination of the Primary Fellowship was given. The college was in Grafton Street. The city itself is beautiful and dynamic, especially on Saturdays when many Irish people come to the bars and celebrate, though the reason to celebrate does not have to be a strong one. Further from the College was O'Connell Street, which is quite famous. The Liffy River runs along it, and it is said that the beer Guinness is nothing but the water of the Liffy in bottles.

The statue of Nelson, resembling the one in Trafalgar Square in London was in the middle of the street. One Saturday some Irish men who hated the statue, climbed it and removed Nelson's head. After that, the army moved in, and putting protection in the front of all the buildings, blasted out to smithereens.

The walls of the College in the front were pockmarked with surface depressions, a result of bullets being fired from muskets during the Irish rebellion. It is a black mark against the British as it was said that the Black and Tans, who were convicts, were given muskets and sent to Ireland to kill the Irish in the uprising.

As soon as Govind started his course in Dublin, the workers at the various banks in the city started a strike. The strike stretched and stretched for months. It seemed that no one was interested in settling the strike. Only in Ireland, eh! It led to enormous hardships for everyone as there was no way one could withdraw money.

❨ ❧0❧ ❩

CHAPTER 79

❖

Mrs. Dunn

Mrs. Dunn's house was to be Govind's residence during the months while he was at the College, where he was a paying guest. The house was in Donnybrook, one of the suburbs of Dublin. Govind took his car to Ireland, as it seemed to be very necessary in his travel to the College, and also go to other areas where he could follow his studies.

Mrs. Dunn was an ill kempt woman of over eighty years. She was dressed in black—dress, sweater etc. and they all looked as they could do with a good wash. Her hair quite often was not brushed, and there were bits of food stuck around her lips. Her mouth spluttered as she talked.

'I tell you, Govind', as she pokes her finger into Govind's chest rather heavily, 'I tell you, America by destiny has Irish Presidents, like the family of the Kennedys. When he goes, there will still be another Irish President', as she pokes him again and again with her heavy dirty fingers. She was obviously obsessed with it.

At one time Dinbala along with the children came over for a visit. Mrs. Dunn took an instant dislike of the visitors. She told Dinbala that Anita would go blind, as she had all that fuzzy curly hair all over her face, stopping her from seeing. It was the last straw when on Sunday the family started to wash the car. According to her it was a sacrilege, and the family had to stop it immediately. The family left soon afterwards. Mrs. Dunn thought that the family was intrusive, and Govind was her possession.

Studies went apace. There were teachers like Drs. Kane, Lynch etc. that taught in the various subjects of Anatomy, Physiology, Pathology, Histology, Biochemistry, Organic Chemistry etc. The courses were very intensive, and the lectures went on throughout the day. Returning home after the day was over with the college, the dinner was consumed rapidly and then it was a return to the books. To learn proper Anatomy, Govind bought a big board on which he attached all the pictures and drawings on the subject (pictures from Last's Surgical Textbook, Grant's Atlas of Anatomy, drawings by Jamieson Evans, Gray's and Cunningham's textbooks of Anatomy etc.). He had a binocular attached to his eyes, and after reading a certain page, he pointed to the area with a long pointer he had in his hand. It certainly made the picture very clearly in the mind.

While pursuing the course, a man called Govind Kini, who was also taking the same course, befriended him. He used to be a demonstrator in Anatomy in Bombay. His knowledge was extensive, and he would be 'a walk through' in the forthcoming examination. Govind and Kini often drove to the seaside to cram the Samson-Wright book in Physiology. Kini's grasp on each page that he read was phenomenal, and he was very good in getting all the facts right. At the beginning of the book, it says 'Rabbi Akiba to his favorite student Simon Ben Kanzai, 'My son, more than the cow wishes to suck, does the cow wish to suckle''. How profound!

Examination time came. The same examination was given in Edinburgh, London, and, of course, Dublin. Most of the examinees that came had failed it in the past, both in Dublin, and elsewhere. Some of them even a few times! It appeared that nobody had passed it the first time. There was a girl who had failed 17 times! She could not sleep the night before and took sleeping tablets, and was late for the exam. and needless to say she did not pass. There was one student who was failed by Professor Kane because he did not say that the Respiratory Center in the Midbrain has its own rhythm.

The results came, and surprise surprise, Govind had passed! That also taking it at the first time! A feat tgat is almost impossible to achieve. It was also disappointing that Kini did not take the exam. Because he thought he would not pass, he did not bother to take the exam. He took it six months later and passed with flying colors. He is now a consultant Orthopedic Surgeon in the south of England. He paid a visit to Govind in Canada at one time.

Govind did it. He ran home to the house owned by Mrs. Dunn, who had kept his dinner waiting. It consisted of two burnt sausages, and some potato. She had left these in the oven all afternoon. Govind was disgusted, and said goodbye to her immediately. He collected his stuff, and left to go home. Unfortunately, there was a strike by the ferry workers, and all the ferries from Dublin to Liverpool had stopped. He drove overnight to Northern Ireland. The highway was good, but it was late at night and it was also foggy. There was a rabbit on the road, and he had to drive behind it, as it just kept running in the center for a long distance. He took the ferry from Larne, to Stranra, the latter being a town in Scotland. From there he drove down to Liverpool, to start life anew once again in the city that was home.

◀ ❧ 0 ❧ ▶

ENGLAND

CHAPTER 80

Back to St. Paul's

O nce again, Govind applied for a job at the Eye Hospital, but this time as a registrar, which is a rung up the ladder that disappears into the sky, metaphorically speaking. He was accepted as the junior registrar, and did two years of the job, except that the status was better and he was given more responsibility. His immediate superior was Sir Malcolm Hutt.

Once there was a child who was scheduled for surgery. The child had Retinoblastoma, and the eye had to be removed. After detaching all the muscles, one has to remove the eye, making sure to obtain the optic nerve as much of its length as possible, as the tumor goes along the nerve to the brain and causes havoc, eventually causing the demise of the child. The Eye was removed, after the gentleman being informed, and waiting for some time for him, which was often rather frustrating as he had a habit of keeping all waiting whenever and wherever he was required. He appeared after the operation was over and was miffed that no one waited for him, which was in fact not true. His pomposity was getting the better of him. He was that form of the pompous character because he was English, and had obtained early knighthood because of the research he had done on the angle structure of the eye in Glaucoma. Govind came across him some years later in Canada where he was head of the Department of Ophthalmology in Salmon Arms, British Columbia, Canada.

The year passed and the job was once again coming to an end. At the same time a job was advertised for a Senior Registrar in the Cheshire Group of Hospitals. None of the Doctors at the Hospital wanted to apply for the job as they thought it was below their dignity to work in the area that was advertised. Govind applied, and who should be the interviewer but Mr. Hopkins! Govind thought he was certain to get the job, and, in fact he did.

CHAPTER 81

A Three Wheeler (I S E T T A)

The Cortina was sold to one of the family members and it was time to get a new car. The family had gone to Mombasa for a visit. A three-wheeler car was advertised. Govind went to see it and was thrilled by it. It cost only twenty five pounds to buy, which was cheap even in those days, and he bought it. There was some engine trouble in that it was hard to start. He found an old Greek chap in town who fixed the problem, and the engine worked like a 'bomb' after that.

The car was interesting. There were two wheels in the front and one behind. It was called a 'bubble' car. The door was in the front, and on opening the door, the steering column that was attached to the door would get out of the way. There was only one seat, which took in three people. They were seated in a row. The engine was on the side at the back. It was rather small. The car was not safe on the big highways, as it was small and somewhat smaller on the major highways, becoming a hazard. It was fun driving the car. Many people had the pleasure of being passengers and have a ride in it. Some nurses also took a ride in this car, and one of the nurses called Sandra Diamont thought she had become romantically involved with the owner. It was embarrassing for Govind to work in the Hospital after giving her a ride in the car. The girl was ubiquitous, and like willow the wisp, to be seen everywhere. It was a relief for Govind when his job expired and he had to move on to another area of the country once again.

CHAPTER 82

Move to Upton-by-Chester

As the job in Liverpool came to an end, the house was put on the market and sold easily. It seems like everyone wanted to live on Queen's Drive, and the house was like a museum. Unfortunately, Govind had the habit of telling the would-be buyers of all the defects in the house, and was eventually told by other members of the family to stay away when people who came to see it.

A house that was newly built was bought in the above village. It was on 28 Gatesheath Drive. The gas heater for water was in the master bedroom. It had two switches, one for heating the water for washing, and the other one was for heating larger volume of water when someone wished to have a bath etc. Here Sheila was useful, and ran up and down to adjust the switches depending on what was required.

Govind bought a brand new Austin38 Saloon, and Dinu bought a Mini Austin Van. Vans were cheaper, especially if they did not have any side windows except for the ones on the doors. One did not have to pay tax on the purchase if a view of the sides was blanked out! It was red in color and she was very happy with it.

CHAPTER 83

A Television

Govind went to Liverpool one day and bought a nice black and white television. It worked well, and Dinu put a vase with flowers on top of it. The Vase contained water in it. Sheila went to reach for something behind the TV on day and the vase toppled over. Water got into the TV and it stopped working. A visit to TV repair shop was made, and Govind explained the problem with regards to the water spilling in it. After an examination, he was told that the TV was irreparable. Govind drove to the city and took it back to the TV shop where he had bought it. He did not tell them about the mishap. He was told to come back in one hour, which he did, and the TV was repaired and in working order once again! All were happy.

CHAPTER 84

Dinu at Deva Hospital

Deva Hospital was for patients with mental disorders. These places tended to be large, and this particular one had 5000 beds! Dinbala applied to work there and was accepted. It was interesting in that the job involved changing the bed sheets, and performing related functions. The ward she worked on had 60 beds. She would start changing the beddings and go all around, and by the time she had finished, it was time to go home, and start the same again the next day. She refused to work there after slaving there for one week.

The next job involved a drive of about 12-Miles to a hospital, which was a sanatorium at one time. She would work all night, then come home, and get all the children sorted out before going to bed herself. The nursery and the school nearby were good. It was hard work, but she eventually obtained a job as a district nurse, which she enjoyed very much, and continued her chosen vocation till the family left for Canada. The patients were very grateful for her work and really appreciated it. It was uncommon for her to come home with some cake or other presents. She was beaming with happiness at finding such a great job. She belonged to the organization known as the VON or Victorian Order of Nurses. The dress was navy blue, with dark Nylon stockings, and a navy blue hat, and dark clean shoes. She was at this job for some years. The hat was cute, and was worn at an angle.

The children went to school in Upton.

Upton zoo was nearby and every night one could hear the roaring of lions, the trumpeting of elephants etc. Chester was about two miles away, where Govind's work was concentrated. The other hospital he had to attend to was Clatterbridge Hospital, about ten miles away. It was the hospital, which also had the Cyclotron, which was used in the treatment of patients with cancer.

CHAPTER 85

◄❧o❧►

Work in Cheshire

The job involved working in Chester Royal Infirmary, and Clatterbridge Hospitals. Ii involved working in the Outpatient Clinics as well as performing surgery in the Operating Room in these places.

While Govind was the senior registrar, his junior was a doctor called Dr. Yousuff. He was a very intense man who came to the clinic earlier than anybody, and because of this fact he looked down on everybody, as most of whom came much later. He was from Pakistan. He was also sore because of the fact that he did not have 'the Primary' despite having taken it a few times. Because of it, he would not obtain the job that was advertised. He was also unhappy because another man of his color was his superior.

The clinics were something else—in one morning they would have booked about sixty patients, making it was impossible to see all the patients properly, and just to make work lighter, many were told to continue with their eye medications. There was only one Slit Lamp (or a biomicroscope, which is used to examine the eye properly). Hence one would have to line up if one wished to use it. It was impossible as one could not waste so much time, and as a consequence the patients obviously did not receive fair treatment.

Going to Clatterbridge involved going through a village called 'Thornton Hough' said to be the most beautiful village in the north. Because of the distance, Govind was given a travel allowance, the money of which was better than his salary, which tended to be meager.

Clatterbridge is an old sanatorium, with low flat buildings all spread out. The operating room was quite far from the eye ward, and the patients were taken to the O.R. by the orderlies in the manner similar to the way the patients were transported in a war zone!

As soon as Govind started the job, he noticed that he had quite a few patients whose maladies he was not quite sure of and looked for advice from his superiors only to find that he was solely responsible for them. He could not obtain the needed advice. However, in all fairness, he was supported in all the decisions he made, whether they were correct or not.

CHAPTER 86

Chester

C hester is the city with a history of over 2000 Years. It was invaded by the Romans who settled there, and built a wall around the City, which is in existence today. The wall is complete, with an amphitheatre on its western end. There are several gift shops as well as restaurants along the wall. For some distance, it runs along the river Dee. Shopping in town is like no other in Britain or elsewhere in that the shops are above a row of shops below. The businesses above are complete with a walkway, while the one below has their own shaded walkway. Interspersed are steps to go to the open corridors above.

Traffic congestion has increased enormously downtown, and because of that, there is a ban to all traffic going downtown except for the ones providing essential services.

CHAPTER 87

❁

Bangor—North Wales

As time went on, the family realized that another source of income was necessary. Eye specialists could earn extra money by working in optical shops, and examine people's eyes, and give a prescription for glasses. It was a lucrative service, as the payment from the government for each patient was 21 Pounds. Govind had Tuesday afternoons off, so he looked for and found a place to provide the service. Unfortunately, it was in Bangor, North Wales, which was a quite a distance away. One had to go through the town of Caernarvon to reach there. The traffic often was bad, especially going through the center of the city mentioned where the bridge was rather narrow, causing a bottleneck. He worked for a few weeks in Bangor, but there was a fly in the ointment. A Dr. Sharma, who was a consultant in the area, phoned him and told him to stop the practice there as it would reduce his chances of becoming a consultant in the future. Govind stopped going to Bangor but was hurt that his own countryman was jealous discouraging him, when he was trying to make a decent living.

There was a man once who had come via the emergency Dept., and was known to have a metallic foreign body in his eye, and even after the knowledge Dr. Yousuff let him go home. When Govind returned from Clatterbridge, he learnt of this, and he immediately went to the X-Ray Dept., saw the films, and called the man back from his home, and proceeded to remove the piece of metal from the patient's eye on the same evening. It certainly did not speak too well for Dr. Yousuff.

The two-year job in Chester was coming to an end, when Mr. Hopkins told him that he should now look for a job as a senior registrar in a teaching Hospital.

Govind applied at St. Paul's once again and had the interview with Mr. Davidson, who asked him as to why he wanted the job at the Hospital. Mr. Davidson was the consultant at the hospital, and Govind had in fact worked under him. Govind told him that it was mainly because it was required for him to work at a teaching Hospital. On further questioning, he was asked if he wanted the job to gain more experience, or for further learning etc. Govind's reply was blunt and told him that for experience Chester job was better, and as for learning, St. Paul's was no better, and often one had to acquire the necessary knowledge through books. It was no wonder that he did get the job.

He was then invited to an interview at Birmingham and Midland Eye Hospital. They had 18 applicants, and short-listed 6 for the interview. Govind went for the interview but knew he would not get the job as some of the candidates were from Birmingham, and would be favored for the job. He later applied to Leeds University Hospital, and was called for an interview.

To go to Leeds, when has to go through the miserable, foggy, featureless land, which has no man or beast, called the Yorkshire Moors (Where Myra Hindley and her partner carried out gruesome crimes against children. She murdered them, and buried them in the area). Govind drove to the moors and reached the town of Huddersfield, and stopped at a coffee house, and after some reflection, decided that he did not want the job. He turned round and went home. The family saw the car coming in the driveway, when someone in the family remarked that the car was coming, and the other member of the family said that it was because of the fact that Govind drove very fast at times!

He had applied to Croydon and Greenwich area Hospital and was called for an interview. However, there was an English person also there, and he had the job. About a month later, Govind was invited once again for an interview there, as one of the consultants had died, and he was sure of the job. However, he told them that he did not want the job as he had decided to go to CANADA, where he had already been for a visit.

CANADA

CHAPTER 88

◀ ❧o❧ ▶

A visit to CANADA

Dr. Smith visited the family in Chester. He was originally from Scotland, where he had qualified as a Doctor, and also did his post-graduate training there. His family now lived in Churchill, Manitoba. It was exciting to talk with him, as, in his practice, he flew all over the country, to places like Flynn Flonn, Churchill and other places, with exciting and exotic names. It seemed he was only checking for glasses but did not carry out any surgery. He said he lived with his family on acreage, and the winters were so cold that life was a little hard at times. There were many moose in the area, so they just hunted one, and hanged the dead animal on a tree with its hind legs, and whenever they felt like some meat, they would just go out with a knife and get a chunk from it as it was hanging outside! It was unbelievable. He even offered an airline ticket to Govind to go and see his place, but Govind declined. However, he was getting restless and did not wish to work any further in The National Health Service in Britain, which he thought was rather stifling. He had a talk with Mr. Hopkins, who had relatives in Iowa, U.S.A. and had visited Toronto. He did not care for Toronto, but thought Govind should go there and look around. If he did, he should go and see the owners of Imperial Optical Company, a firm that was Canada wide. Govind made a resolve then and there that he would travel and see personally this exciting country.

Dinbala purchased a ticket for him to fly to New York, and then he was to take the Greyhound to Toronto, and then the train that was called The Canadian National, to Calgary. He was to fly back in two weeks from Calgary. In New York he was to confirm his return seat with the same airline.

The flight to New York was uneventful. He took a cab into town. They were the yellow cabs that New York is famous for, but most of them were dilapidated junks. They seem to be very busy, but they did not appear to be respecter of people's luggage as they really manhandled them. He spent an afternoon walking around the city with an Australian gentleman, who was also visiting the place at the same time. In Australia they also drive their cars on the left hand side, so, on crossing the road, there is a tendency for the new comers to look the wrong way, i.e. to the right instead of left. Govind saved his life a few times, pulling him back at the right time. The traffic lights were impressive, as they ordered you to 'WALK', or 'DON'T WALK'.

Govind boarded the Greyhound and expected it to go at a breakneck speed, but it never went over 55 Miles and Hour, much to his disappointment and chagrin. However, it was impressive that there was a separate lane for buses only! The bus reached Buffalo, where it stopped for a while. He had some coffee there, and he was asked if he wanted cream in his coffee, but he replied that milk would do, as the cream could be extra money, so he thought!

The first problem arose in New York. On calling the company, he was told that his return should have been confirmed three weeks ago! All along his travel, he made repeated calls to the airline, to be told the same thing. It was rather frustrating. In the end, he had to buy another ticket for his return, which left him bankrupt.

In Toronto, he met an austere Indian gentleman called Mr. Dilip Pithadia; somewhat tall, with a black shirt, and pants that coordinated and complimented the shirt, with a pipe in his mouth, though it never appeared to be lit, and it looked as though it was there to impress people. He also had the annoying habit to say after every sentence 'Do you follow me?' or 'Do you understand?', as though all those that were listening could not follow his brilliant exposé. His wife was Dinbala's friend from the old country of East Africa, though she lived in Tanganyika (now Tanzania, after Tanganyika amalgamated with the Island of Zanzibar), whereas the old girl was from Mombasa. Dinu's grandpa was in Dar-Es-Salaam. The charming lady's name was Usha. Usha met him at the station as her husband was still working. The two of them took the train to Misessauga, one of the suburbs of Toronto. Govind took a lot of photographs of this pleasant lady, without realizing that the camera had no film in it!

The first problem arose when he went to the bathroom. Nowhere on the door was a stopper. He used the bathroom with trepidation. Next day he went in the shower, and had the same ill feelings, as he would have loved to lock the bathroom while he was using it. Only afterwards he learnt that the lock was a part of the door handle!

Driving around in Toronto in the evening was very interesting. It was raining heavily, but the drivers of all the vehicles did not slow down at all. Many cars were slipping and sliding, but that did not deter them! Some went down the ditch; others went in circles on the road, but recovered and continued with their careless dangerous driving. Govind thought, 'Wow, the wild west is here!'

He took a walk along the main streets of Toronto, and he saw the sign of Imperial Optical Company on a two story building in Dundas Square. He decided to go upstairs on the second floor where the main office was located. He told the girl who was on the switchboard that he was a Doctor who was visiting from Britain. As soon as she heard the word 'Doctor' she stood up in reverence. She contacted a Mr. Casson who passed on a message that he was at a meeting, but wondered if Govind cared to return in an hour. So Govind went away and came back in one hour. On his return, the girl stood up again—wow, what a reception! Thought Govind. He had a long talk with Mr. Casson, who told him about Ophthalmic Practices, Schooling for children, etc. etc. in Canada. They also kept a list of the areas where Ophthalmologists were most needed. He informed Govind that a town in Alberta called Red Deer was badly in need of an ophthalmologist. The town was about fifty miles from a city called Calgary. Beautiful lakes surrounded the town. He was introduced to a Mr. Cecil Oostenbrug, who had an optical outlet in Calgary. Cecil impressed Govind that he should explore the Calgary area. Mr. Oostenburg told him that if he decided to go to Calgary, he would have his son in law called Christopher Temoshawski pick him up, and show him the area. Not only that, but he would pay for Govind's stay at a hotel.

Govind had an appointment to see a Dr. Bowerman in Oshawa, the town being close to Toronto, where GM cars are manufactured. He went and saw him and his wife, but did not think he would like to work in the town. Next day he took the train which was to go to Calgary.

The train started at 4p.m.; the view from his window at all the greenery as well a myriad of colors on all the trees was breathtaking and was impressed with the grandeur of the land. (He was in Canada in October, when it is autumn). In the Indian language the season is called 'Pankher', which literally means 'falling leaves'. In the evening he had dinner, and enquired about the countryside, when he was told that he was still in Ontario. He woke up in the morning, and enquired again, and he was told that he was still in Ontario. 'Wow, just how big is this country?' he thought. The train was the most beautiful train he had ever seen. On leaving the station it goes through a wash! It has beautiful dining cars, and some of the carriages even have an upstairs dome, which is all glass. There is music playing as one watches out of the window as the train travels the beautiful country. Even flat lands like the prairies of Saskatchewan are impressive in that there is not a man or beast to be seen. They say that if a dog runs away from home, he can be seen for three or four days. The reason they say for his running away is that he is in fact looking for a tree! The train went through Manitoba with the towns having exotic names derived from the appearances of the jaw of a moose, or a hat that is full of Medicines! (Rudyard Kipling visited Medicine Hat three times. He loved the name.) Winnipeg was gone by, and the city of

Regina was reached. Govind had an interview in the city, but did not have the heart to stop and go for the interview, mainly because of the flat and featureless land. At the station was the statue of a boy, with a sheaf of wheat in his hands. It was golden in color and very impressive. On and on the train went, and on the third day, Calgary had arrived.

As promised, Chris. Temoshawski was there at the station. He took Govind to Calgary Inn. It was a beautiful hotel in downtown Calgary, and very comfortable indeed. He ordered great breakfasts in the mornings, with coffee cup filled up for any number of times. He had never in his life seen before. He did not realize that the price of breakfast was not included in overnight stays, the mistake for which he paid dearly.

Christopher appeared early in the morning the next day, and said he could drive Govind to the town of Red Deer if he wanted. Govind agreed eagerly. They drove on the highway on the wrong side, according to Govind. They went through several villages, and reached the town eventually. An optician called Steve Huber met them. His optical shop is famous in the area. He was somewhat of an anxious man, having trouble in mastering English, having come from Germany. In later life he was divorced, and married twice more. One of the ladies, Sandra was the divorced wife of a minister of the church! Sandra had her cosmetic surgery to her eyelids, breast implants, her teeth done, and then left him. He was stuck with big bills as well as two young children!

Govind saw a mannequin in one of the shopping malls in Calgary, about 8 Feet tall, dressed up as a Cowboy, and the caption said: 'Give a little more, feel a little bigger'. It sure felt good just to read that.

In Red Deer, he was shown a building that was being built. He was told that he could have his office there if he wanted. It was on the second floor of The Royal Bank Building. The office could be the area facing east, or the one facing north. Govind said that it did not matter as to what area he occupied. Then the journey next day was to Edmonton, where he saw the Registrar to the College of Physicians and Surgeons. He filled out the necessary forms, and was registered immediately, and was told to start practice in Alberta immediately if he wished, but as a general practitioner and not as a specialist, for which he would have to pass Canadian examinations.

There was only one problem as the two drove on, which, according to Govind, was minor, but according to Chris, major, and that was that the engine in his car kept heating up, and he worried about it all the way to Edmonton and back. However, he did not check the engine and put some water in, which might have helped more!

On his return, Govind booked to travel back to Britain, the plane was to land in Manchester. By now he was totally broke, so he made a collect call to his wife in Chester and told her to be sure to collect him from the airport in Manchester, as he had no money.

CHAPTER 89

Goodbye National Health Service and Chester

He had taken many photographs of the countryside, as well as the houses in Red Deer, which he showed to the family rather proudly, and they were all impressed. That very evening he wrote a letter of resignation and asked Sheila, his daughter to go the village and mail it. The notice was to take effect in three months, when he would end his job. Dinbala had to quit her job. The family dog called Prince was taken over by a farmer. Someone asked 'Have you told the dog yet that you are off to Canada'. That dog was good at causing problems! Once he jumped out of a car when it stopped at traffic lights, and it was a job to find him. At another time he went into the neighbors' home. He proceeded to gulp down a packet of butter and a loaf of bread that was lying on the table! Later in the evening Janet and Eric were arguing with some heat, as she was adamant that she had left lunch out for him, and he was miffed as it was not there when he was came home.

A new home was found for the dog and he was left there one day, but on the next day he was back again. He ran back home and found his way all the way back!.

One of the neighbors, when he heard that the family was to go to Canada, said that even he would go only if he was younger. And he was 39!

CHAPTER 90

Goodbye Britain

Then the hectic business of winding up in Chester began. Govind acquired wooden boxes, three feet by three feet by three feet, and all the essentials were put in it and shipped to the Optician in Red Deer. There were nineteen boxes! The two cars were sold away, one to his nephew, and the beautiful new car, a 4 Door one, again an Austin to his brother Maganlal. Many household items were sold as a form of Garage sale. Even the special picture was gone. It was that of a Spanish boy, poor, wearing a straw hat, and tears rolling down his face. On seeing it, one felt like taking him in his arms, wipe off his tears and hug him and never let him go! The house itself was put on the market, and was sold about a year later for nine thousand pounds, about eighteen thousand dollars.

The family decided to go to Kenya once again before proceeding to Canada. However, after buying the tickets to Kenya, there was no money left over to go to Canada from England. Once again Nanjibhai was useful as he was kind enough to purchase the ticket for the family to proceed to Canada. Damjibhai, Govind's father-in-law, was also kind enough to give the family a sum of 110 American Dollars as a present, the money that he had saved in his business.

CHAPTER 91

❮❥᪣0᪢❯

Canada

Life begins in Red Deer

At last the family arrived in Canada. They flew into the City of Calgary airport. Chris was at the airport, and offered a ride for the whole family to Red Deer. It was late in the afternoon when the family went through the town, and stopped at a coffee shop north of the town.

Dinbala thought that there was enough time, and Chris could show the town to the family if he wished. 'What town?' said he, 'we just drove through it!' Realizing what a small town it was, the family was disappointed, and it showed on their faces! The family was taken to The Blue Pine Motel, which was at the East End of town. There was a huge mound of snow in the backyard where the children had loads of fun. The family had no car or other modes of transport.

It was a Sunday, but milk was needed for the children. No problem, Govind thought, he will just walk down to the shops and buy it. He walked and walked. It was cold, bitter cold, the likes of which he had never seen in his life. As he went along, a truck stopped for him, and offered him a ride, which he took eagerly. He reached the shops to find that it being Sunday, they were closed. Another lift from another kind driver in a truck that offered him a ride back, and he took it. Time and again he was to see the kindness and friendliness of all the people of this country—they have as big a heart as the size of the country, which is very big! Much bigger than you can imagine!

There were signs all over in town asking you to come and borrow money. It was unbelievable. Govind borrowed money and bought a brand new turquoise Datsun. It was a beautiful car, but now and then the engine stopped. After some time he realized that that was because the gas cap was so tight that there was a tremendous vacuum created in the gas tank. All he had to do was to open out the cap and it worked. He had to do it quite often

The family rented a house. The local eye specialist's wife, Joan was so kind that she supplied the sofas and curtains for the house. After some time, Dr. William McPeek, the other eye specialist that practiced in the town, announced that he was going to give free service in Afghanistan and would leave Canada for three months. He left all his workload to Govind. Govind got busy from the first day he started! His being busy went on for thirty years.

After about ten years, he moved his office to another building that was a fourplex that he owned. The two apartments downstairs were converted into a large office for examining and treating some eye disorders that needed minor surgery.

Thirty years passed like the blink of an eye. There were many eye disorders that were seen and treated. These included Cataracts, Glaucoma, Ocular Inflammations of all kinds, many of them having to be taken to the hospital for treatment and even an operation performed urgently if it was considered necessary.

CHAPTER 92

A Cottage

G ovind bought a cottage by the lake. The family had many hours of fun at the cottage, where Anita became an expert at water skiing. The cottage also had an outdoors sauna. It was great to have a sauna there and then go out and roll in the snow. Often the family took the boat out and went unto the town, which was about 12 Miles away, just for an ice cream! It was fun to cross country sky on the lake. The small dog they had also jumped along like a rabbit as he accompanied the revelers. The fire in the cottage was lit, and some good meals were had there. Many of his friends also visited them.

CHAPTER 93

Kirti

In the town of Red Deer was born the last of the four children. She was called Kirti, which means kindness, and that is exactly what she was. Always chatty, and loving, with bright eyes, and a mind like a computer that was working at a breakneck speed. Anyone who came across her endeared her, and remembered her forever. She finished school and went to the University of Calgary, where she finished with honors. She became the main writer for speeches for Mr. John Mills, a member of parliament that originated from the same town. His meteoric rise to power and become the Deputy Prime Minister of Canada was in no small measure to the extremely richly worded and powerful speeches she wrote for him.

CHAPTER 94

⟨ ❧ o ☙ ⟩

Brain tumor

For about five years Govind had problems with his health. He felt that all was not well but was unable to put his finger on the dilemma. The symptoms were rather ill defined and not even present continuously. It was not incapacitating. It started with annoying sounds in the Right ear in the form of a continuous hissing noise, generally constant in its pitch.

Sometimes there was another noise that was quite distinct from the first one. Eventually it became so bad that he had to leave the radio on all night by his bedside. The radio had to be quite loud, so that it would drown out the other noises that were in his Brain. While working at his cottage, when he put the dock out onto the lake, which he had to do at the end of every winter season, he could not see straight to drive in the nails while hammering. On looking at the lake, he would see a shimmer and he would feel dizzy.

Later on he started to have headaches. He made an appointment to see his family Doctor, a gentleman called Dr. Crawford, who was an emigrant from Glasgow, Scotland. Dr. Crawford lacked the expertise for a full neurological examination. His fingers were shaky. However he was always very friendly and courteous. He checked Govind for his eye movements etc. but could not reach a conclusion with regards to his problems.

However, he knew his limitations, and referred Govind to a neurologist. The nerve specialist was a Dr. Richard Grieves. A short thin man, very intense, he always carried a little black bag with him wherever he went. He was very thorough in his examination and tests, and concluded that Govind was showing signs of aging. Govind continued to work, and even perform Cataract Surgeries where he had no problems.

He later on started having nystagmus, which is an oscillatory movement of the eyes whereby objects appear to have a to and fro movements as one watches them. He saw an E.N.T. Specialist, a Dr. Weir, who was also not conclusive as regards to the diagnosis. The problems continued for some years.

Once, Govind did a locum in a place called Tabuk, Saudi Arabia. There he saw many patients and even performed cataract surgeries.

There was a Dr. Roy in the place at the same time. He was also doing a locum, and had come from Britain. He did a lot of ear surgeries on children, many of them needed to have a small hole made in the Tympanic membrane in the ear. It was to release the pent up fluid or pus in the middle ear, and insert a tube in the hole that was made surgically to keep it open for some time.

Before the surgeries, he did audiometric tests, some of which was to introduce sound waves in the affected ear and recording responses on a graph. Govind requested his friend if he would do the same test on him. He agreed and performed the test. The response was very marked and rather odd in that the needle went all the way down the paper and left it. Whatever it was, the disease must be quite severe to show what it did! Dr. Roy said that he had never seen anything like it, so Govind just took a photocopy of the same and asked the experts in Red Deer to look at it, and they expressed a similar opinion and said the same thing, admitting that they had never seen anything like it and did not know what it meant! The town of Red Deer had a C.A.T. Scanner installed in1982, and a request was made for Govind to have it done on him.

The next day after the test, Dr. Grieves called Govind's office, and asked the secretary as to what time the office closed. He was informed that it would close at 4 p.m. He asked the secretary to tell Govind to come to his office as soon as he closed his office. Govind went to see him as soon as his office closed.

'I AM AFRAID YOU HAVE A BRAIN TUMOR' said he. It seemed heartless, as Govind should have had his wife there for support. But Govind had to have a brave face, which he did. He went home, and the family was having a party. 'I guess he told that you have a Brain tumor', said the wife jokingly. 'I am afraid he did' said he, as he broke down. The room went deathly quiet as it took some time to have the fact sink in.

At least a firm diagnosis had reached, as his headaches were getting worse, especially in the early mornings. He would start pacing the floor at that time with no relief in sight. He was referred to a Brain Surgeon, a Dr. Michael Hunter in Calgary. Further CAT Scans were done, to confirm the fact that it was what was called an Acoustic Nuroma. It is a benign tumor, and once removed does not come back, so he said. 20 Percent of postmortems done on people who have died of other causes have acoustic nuromas!

The good Doctor performed surgery successfully in Calgary, and Govind came home to recuperate. He had good insurance, and the insurance company paid the amounts as per the contract every month, tax free, in the ensuing period. He found it difficult to stay at home and do nothing, and, after a while, as he could not stand it, he went back to work after staying off work for about six months.

Time passed rapidly with all that work in his busy office. After about two years, his symptoms started to return. He started to see the hospital double as he approached it, although it was transitory. He could not walk straight, and had to get a support from the walls as he went along. He made another appointment with Dr. Grieves, who was not sure as to what was happening. He was referred back to Dr. Michael Hunter. His CAT Scans were repeated, and it was thought that the tumor was enlarging again. It was suggested that he should go and see a Dr. Charles Tator in Toronto, as he had performed surgeries on over three hundred patients who had this kind of tumor. Alberta Health Care was very good. It paid for him and his wife to fly out and see the Doctor in Toronto, for the first visit (It was called 'Air Ambulance' by the service), and later once again for the surgery. Dr. Tator measured the tumor and compared the sizes from previous films and came to the conclusion that the tumor had enlarged. Tests on the Seventh nerve, which is closely associated with the Eighth Nerve, or the so-called Auditory Nerve from which the tumor grows, were performed. The test is to map out the Seventh Nerve so that an inadvertent incision of the Nerve can be avoided during surgery. All patients who have surgery for this form of tumor have distorted faces as this nerve has to be cut quite often to remove the tumor. The distortion that the tumor causes the brain as it grows is unbelievable. It pushes the Brain aside for more than inch or an inch and a hRodney!

The tumor was the size of a plum. It can also block the flow of Cerebrospinal fluid, which circulates in and around the Brain and Spinal Cord, causing acute headaches and eventual death from coning of the Brain into the narrow Spinal canal. However, he had another successful surgery, and the tumor was removed totally. Removing the tumor the first time had taken 9 Hours, and the next time it was 11 Hours! You have got to admire those surgeons who work patiently for such long hours on their feet!

Once again, Insurance money started rolling in and it could have gone on until he was 65! However, six months passed and Govind wished to restart his office. He interviewed a number of girls to act as secretary but none appeared to be satisfactory, until Pearl Church came to the office for an interview.

Pearl had worked in an optometrist's office and was willing to learn in a similar line of work. She was also in the middle of a divorce, and had to prove to the authorities that she had a good steady job, as she could easily support the three children she had. She was hired immediately as she appeared to be a great asset, as it also turned out to be. Her social life was fantastic. She was very active in her personal life. Busy arranging for parties, a wedding or a golf game etc. She loved jewelry on her hands, and her nails were long, which were awkward when she assisted in the minor surgeries that Govind performed in the office. However, in fairness, she was meticulous with regards to maintaining a sterile field in surgery. She knew many people, and most of them came in the office for eye examinations. Her divorce went through, and she met a fireman who was also a hockey star and played with the Calgary Flames. He went on to making millions as time went on. He became quite rich, and even though Pearl did not have to work for money, she continued to work until Govind retired and sold the office.

It was on his return after the surgery that the problems really started. Some of the medical staff disliked Govind and saw an opportunity to keep him from renewing his privileges at the Hospital. Govind threatened to sue the hospital if he would not get his privileges back. It was decided that he should undergo neuropsychological examination. A Dr. Barbara McMillan saw him in Edmonton. A full day was spent in the clinic, with numerous tests for memory, recall, etc. performed. Her report was that Govind had Cognitive Agnosia and surgical privileges should not be granted to him. Besides the surgeries, he could continue with his normal practice.

Govind went and saw a Dr. King in Calgary, who was of a similar opinion, that there was a hemispheric defect, i.e. in the brain in the form of a cognitive agnosia, but he did not think this would affect the work as an ophthalmologist. Govind communicated with Dr. Hunter and Dr. Tator, both of whom thought that it was a storm in a teacup and they did not understand all the fuss being made about a return of his privileges at the hospital, and they thought that his privileges must be restored to him and that also immediately, including surgical privileges. Medical staff had another meeting, and it was approved by a small margin that if another ophthalmologist saw him at two sessions in surgery while he was the surgeon performing the surgery, and the said ophthalmologist approved of his surgery, then he would see a return of his privileges. Approaching the other ophthalmologists in town with regard to the requirement was fruitless.

A Dr. E. Fernanades had started his practice in Edmonton, and he was approached. He was asked if he would be kind enough to travel to Sprit River and see Govind perform the surgeries as was required. Dr. Don Pearson who was the Medical Director was one of the Doctors who wanted to help Govind as much as possible for a return of his surgical privileges, and he turned out to be a gentleman, and a great helper. He was fair and honest and did not wish to take any sides but he was intent on discovering the truth act accordingly. Dr. Fernanades saw him perform the surgeries as was required, and was very positive in his report. Govind did not see the report itself. Hey presto, he had his privileges restored.

❧ ⁓0⁓ ☙

CHAPTER 95

Cataract

In Britain as well as in Canada Govind performed many cataract surgeries. Many improvement occurred in the techniques of the operations itself, starting originally with a large incision and removal of the cataract. It involved the patient having to stay still in bed for a week with sandbags on either side of his head. Later fine sutures were used, and that made it possible to mobilize the patient sooner. However, it was revolutionized when Harold Ridley, in 1948 noted that many aircraft pilots who had injured their eyes with the canopy of the planes had no reaction at all to the Perspex in the eyes. This gave him the idea that a lens of the same material can be made, and introduced in the eye after removal of the cataract. It worked well and many of his patients had this done. Some of these patients are even alive today. The lens has improved today to a remarkable degree. It comes in much smaller sizes, and is even foldable, requiring a much smaller incision to put it in the eye. It then unfolds itself! Even the materials are also different—like Perspex, silicone, etc. Even the methods of removal of the cataract have improved, and lasers, ultrasounds are brought in to use.

Apart from the disease of cataracts, there are numerous other diseases that afflict the Eye. Not only that, but many diseases of the body are manifest in the Eye.

CHAPTER 96

⤜⧽०⧼⤛

Red Deer

The town of Red Deer was caught up in the boom that was in fact in all Alberta. The big gusher that was termed 'black gold' sprouted from the ground when a hole was dug in the ground in Leduc brought in prosperity for the whole country. The Liberal Government of the time was buoyant under the premiership of Mr. Manning. The problem of Benign Spongiform Encephlopathy (or mad cow disease) that affected cattle of the day was conquered. The oil prices went over 40 Dollars a barrel, which was a boon to the government. The country was lucky that the avian flu that affected birds in British Columbia did not spread to the chickens in Alberta. All this helped Alberta develop a prosperous and buoyant economy beyond imagination.

The hospital was in the middle of huge expansion, with a large helipad constructed in front of this mammoth, so that a helicopter was available at anytime to take patients to the cities when and if required.

The eye room was used extensively for eye examinations of many disabled and infirm patients at the hospital. To everyone's chagrin, the room was closed, only to be replaced later with a larger facility that provided all forms of services.

The family doctors and others collected money in the nearby towns of Acme for the hospital in Red Deer so that a laser could be purchased for the eye department at the hospital. The money came, and the administration was able to put the money to good use.

Enter Dr. Samantha Martin, another Ophthalmologist. She was a research assistant in Veterinary Section involved in disorders of the eye at the research dept. of the University of Edmonton. She went on to study ophthalmology and obtained distinction in her exams. She applied and obtained her privileges to work in all areas of ophthalmology at the hospital. She was very bright and an astute businesswoman. Soon afterwards, the hospital was kind enough to buy a laser, which turned out to be a very useful instrument. Services in ophthalmology expanded, and two operating rooms were opened to provide the people of Red Deer and surrounding area of the extended services. Another ophthalmologist joined the hospital, and numerous cataracts were performed. Many diabetics were treated with the laser with excellent results.

CHAPTER 97

Life in Red Deer

O ver the many years, the town grew leaps and bounds. Govind developed an Acoustic Neuroma which was removed successfully, although the legacy of it was a facial palsy. It could make for another story.

The family also increased in their numbers, a result of which was four children and seven grandchildren.

CHAPTER 98

⟨ೞ०ﮩ⟩

Ramnik's family in Nyeri

Ramniklal, the youngest of the five brothers now owns Ladies Tailoring House. His son has also joined him and the business has continued to increase by leaps and bounds.

If you ever go to the small town of Nyeri, you would have to approach it with the ingredients of nostalgia and imagination. The road may be good, but at one time it was just red dirt and occasionally mud, more like the skin of a very old man with cracks, breaks, varying sizes of irregular depressions, but full of its own personality. As you turn right, you will see a school on the right, and if you are lucky, you may see bright eager black intermingles with other ethnic faces, intelligent, and ready to soak in all information given to them, like a sponge. Imagine the same faces being of Indian children from years gone by, progeny of parents who themselves were poor, although pioneers. For apparel, the child may be wearing a shirt, three quarter length khaki shorts, but no shoes. The feet may be cracked and bleeding from the heat and the hard earth. Some may even have the 'dudu', a common parasite that is on the ground, and attacks the foot, making its home under the skin. Going further and turning left, you may imagine shops of the many enterprising Indians.

It is now that you have truly entered the town of Nyeri. Let your imagination go wild! You may see a black giant that has just woken up. He has just sat up. He may be bleary eyed as the dawn is just starting for him. He is unkempt, and his clothes are in tatters. He is staring in an easterly direction. He has the marks of the chains on his hands and feet that he has just broken. The fetters are that of slavery, poverty, disease, and premature death. His clothes are naught but rags, and his hair is all crinkled, windblown and scruffy. He stares into the horizon where the sun is just coming up. It is bright and full of warmth, and you know that it brings a new dawn, the sunrise of hope, health and prosperity. In the horizon are the promises of longevity for all the people that live in this country, the country that was the cradle of humankind when Lucy stood up erect on her feet and started walking with her group. It happened somewhere in this very land, many thousands of years ago.

Passing through the town, and turning left, you will eventually go onto the Ring Road, and see the Outspan Hotel. Imagine a young Princess doing her beautiful and gracious dance in the idyllic surroundings, and the next day, leaving the town a Queen, with all her majesty and might, the greatest Queen the world has ever seen. Sad also to leave this land she loved so much despite her short stay, to be on her way to rule her own mighty country where, on the passing of her father to another world, she is needed immediately and urgently.

At the top of the street, just before you reach the tower, you may see the Post Office on your left. Next to it you may see the Ladies Tailoring House. Enter the shop, and you may meet the owner of the unending dynasty. You may see his two sons, and their wives. You may also see two children who just finished school and came to the store. These are the grandchildren of the owner of the store. Their faces bright and eager, not only that, but you may spot the eternal businessmen in them. On seeing this family, you will see vividly in your mind that although some members of the Bhadresa family have departed this world, but in truth, they have not. You will see them on the faces of these youngsters, and you know that they are getting ready to take up the challenge of this great country, and somewhat unknowingly, continue a dynasty.

And who is that old man, looking at one of the displays in the shop? He appears somewhat lost. And what about that odd uniform he is wearing? Dressed in a scout's hat, khaki jacket, khaki shorts, knee length stockings, and a kerchief tied around his neck. The hat on his head looking a little odd. He has a number of medals proudly worn over his khaki shirt. He has a long staff in his right hand. Attached to his belt around his waist are some well-worn articles—a knife, a compass as well as other paraphernalia. He appears tall, thin and rather muscular, obviously sturdy, impressive, out of the ordinary looking. You feel you want to meet him, and shake his hand and make his acquaintance.

As you approach, he turns around, and you see an uncanny resemblance to a very familiar historical figure that comes to mind. Wait a minute, the hand is that of a man has a slight tremble, but is firm. It is wrinkled heavily and leathery, rather like the skin of a lizard. He takes yours in a vice-grip like handshake. The face becomes clearer as he you approach. There is an aura of greatness about him.

You know now that the extended hand of friendship is that of none other than that of the famous scout, the one and only, the founder of the movement, renowned in all the countries of this world. It can be the hand of the only one, undisputedly, and of *nobody else in world but that of-*

CHAPTER 99

LORD BADEN POWELL OF GILWELL

—LORD ROBERT BADEN POWELL OF GIL

Not unlike the head of the Medusa, a phenomenal outgrowth of questions is sprouting out of your mind:

What is he doing here?

Does he need more converts?

Has he chosen to retire in the beautiful Highlands of Nyeri, rather than his own country of origin? Is it because of this beautiful place and its wonderful people?

You feel your day is made. It is like no other day that has been or ever would be, and you will savor it forever and ever, as you say goodbye to this great man.

◄ ୭o୧ ►

The End

◄ ୭0୧ ► ◄ ୭0୧ ► ◄ ୭0୧ ►

ISBN 0-9737278-0-2

Contact : *govindbhadresa@yahoo.com.* Govind32@hotmail.com